'Ah!' Sam tutted. 'A Career woman.'

'You sound prejudiced, Sam,' Paula answered equably. 'What a pity. I had taken you for a broader-thinking man.'

'I was once,' he retorted with a trace of rare cynicism in his tone. 'But I seem to have come across too many career women to allow my thinking to get much broader.'

Paula lifted her eyebrows. 'Really? And you propose to judge me on previous experience?'

'Experience—and lessons learnt.'

Carol Wood writes her medical romances based on personal experience, backed by her work in medical general practice. Married to a water-colour artist and with three of her children now living on the south coast, she enjoys conservation of wildlife, reading and curio shops.

Recent titles by the same author:

SOMETHING SPECIAL

BY
CAROL WOOD

MILLS & BOON®

*MILLS & BOON and MILLS & BOON with the Rose Device
are registered trademarks of the publisher.*

*First published in Great Britain 1998
Harlequin Mills & Boon Limited,
Eton House, 18-24 Paradise Road, Richmond, Surrey TW9 1SR*

© Carol Wood 1998

ISBN 0 263 80785 1

*Set in Times 10 on 11 pt. by
Rowland Phototypesetting Limited
Bury St Edmunds, Suffolk*

03-9805-50001-D

*Printed and bound in Great Britain
by Mackays of Chatham PLC, Chatham*

CHAPTER ONE

THE second Paula walked through the door, she realized she'd made a mistake—a whopper, as Aunt Steph would say. This was no ordinary, sleepy country practice filled with gently nodding grey heads or shuffling Zimmers as she had expected to find in the tiny Warwickshire village of Struan. The scene which met her astonished grey eyes was more like a set from *Jurassic Park*, with at least two Mr Blobbys—of the stuffed cerise wool variety—whistling across the room to collide with a mixture of pterodactyls and brontosauruses unleashed by at least fifteen screaming under fives.

'Tea's ready in the garden, children!' shouted a strident female voice above the multitude of tiny heads, and the room descended into abrupt and stunning silence.

'OK, scram!' exclaimed another deeper, huskier voice which belonged, it appeared, to the photographer lowering a camcorder slowly in front of him. 'And don't all charge at once.'

Despite the command, Paula found herself flattened against the wall as fifteen hyperactive children, suddenly moved from trance to action, galloped past her and through the door which presumably led to the tuck.

When the last little boy had disappeared after tripping over the mat, bravely picking himself up to thrust his shirt back into his shorts, Paula stared around the battleground of a surgery, over the chairs and magazine racks pushed aside to clear the decks, finally to swing her eyes up into the deep brown irises of the man who held the camera.

'Looking for the party?' He frowned at her, the dark

eyes critically assessing her carefully prepared appearance—the svelte powder-blue suit, pale blonde bobbed hair and fashionable high heels. 'You'd better follow Mrs McDuff,' he told her abruptly. 'She's most of the stuff organized for outside games. You're early, you know.'

He came towards her, looming over the chaos, folding back the untidy black hair which waved down to his denim open-necked shirt and flicked gently across the deeply tanned column of strong throat. Long...very long legs clad in dark blue summer cotton and ending in boating shoes moved towards her, stopping within inches as he bent down, lifted the beast in front of him and whirred away.

'Smile!' he shouted, which of course she did, possibly because she was trapped against the wall with nowhere to go!

She found herself blinking self-consciously under a soft golden wing of hair, which fortunately sheltered huge and lovely grey eyes shyly avoiding a direct contact with the camera's operator.

The camera clicked off.

Paula let out a soft sigh of relief.

The frown on the face—bronzed and attractively weather-worn and with eyes that glittered a deep brown, earthy intensity—deepened sharply. He jerked his head towards the garden. 'Sue will organize you a copy of a video. Don't worry, there'll be enough to go around.'

Paula shook her head. 'Actually, I'm—'

'Off you go!' he shooed her abruptly. 'You won't get eaten alive unless the trifle is soggy. I don't guarantee your clothes, though.' Again the dark eyes went over her suit. 'Personally, I'd have thought something less fussy would have been more appropriate for a kid's birthday party.'

Paula's mouth fell open. Well, she'd seen something

written in those eyes, but she hadn't realized until now it was plain rudeness—and he didn't even know her! He hoisted the camera once more, clamped it safely between two large suntanned hands and began scanning the devastation of the room.

Paula thought that, if he treated his customers as he had her, she rated his chances of success in business a shade less than zero. Once she might have ignored such crass ignorance—before life had taken hold of her and given her a shake in the form of Jay Rolands—now she had no intention of being growled at by anyone, least of all someone whose communication skills seemed to match the size of his lens!

'You're in my line of filming!' he called, one eye screwed up as he swung around. He lowered the camera once more to stare at her. 'I need to film those things!' He gestured irritably to the stuffed animals on the floor.

'And I'm in your way, I suppose?'

'Just move to one side, will you?'

Paula's resolution to keep calm evaporated. This time she looked him up and down with as much scrutiny as he had given her. Common courtesies such as 'please' and 'thank you' obviously never entered his head!

She gave him a withering glare and jumped the trail of toys as elegantly as she could, finally reaching blessed fresh air in the garden with her head held high.

Dr Sue Dunwoody waved to her from the other side of the garden where the children ate at a long trestle table. Paula had met Sue a month ago when she had travelled up from London for the locum interview here at Struan House Surgery. Sue had shown her over the big converted Georgian house which was both home and practice to the married partners, Sue and Ken Dunwoody.

The other doctors had been absent, she remembered; John Linton had been eating a roast with his young wife at the Black Dog in Warwick and Sam Carlile had been away for the weekend in London.

Looking radiant in her fourth month of pregnancy, Sue took Paula's hand and shook it warmly, then waved to Mrs McDuff, who was shovelling popcorn into paper cups. 'Can you manage, Mrs McDuff, just for ten minutes?'

'Go ahead, Dr Dunwoody, we're fine.' Mrs McDuff smiled bravely.

'Mrs McDuff's our live-in housekeeper-cum-nanny and she's a treasure,' Sue told Paula as she led her to a quiet wooden bench to sit down. 'And that's Poppy, the plump one on the grass with the toy dog and twice as much popcorn in her mouth as anyone else. It's her birthday today, as you can see by the chaos. We decided to muster all the children in Reception.' She giggled. 'Needs must, I'm afraid, but the kids seemed to love the idea.'

Paula's gaze lingered on the golden-haired little girl. 'She's gorgeous, Sue. How old is she?'

'Five.' Sue's hazel eyes shadowed as she pushed back her soft brown hair. 'Poppy is a Down's child, Paula. Thought I'd mention it before she comes and plonks herself on your lap and demands immediate attention.'

Paula gazed back at the little girl on the lawn and wondered how on earth Sue coped with a Down's child, a busy practice and the prospect of another child on the way.

Sue sighed. 'Before you ask, I haven't had the triple blood test. I know there's a possibility of another Down's baby or even spina bifida, but, you see, I wouldn't consider a termination even if the baby was at risk. Ken and I hold quite old-fashioned ethical beliefs. We just hope and pray the next one's going to be all right.' She suddenly laughed, waving aside the serious moment. 'Now, how did we get onto this subject? Tell me, how is your aunt, and have you settled in yet?'

Paula dragged her mind back and recalled the hectic week moving into her aunt's ancient old house in Warwick. 'Well, Aunt Steph is great, thanks to the Brufen you started her on. And I've settled into the little flat at the back of her house—but I'm looking forward to tomorrow. . .' she glanced back to the surgery '. . .when hopefully the coast will be clear of rampantly abrasive photographers,' she added ruefully.

Sue frowned. 'Photographers?'

'The camcorder man. My goodness, it's a wonder he hasn't frightened all the kids off. He had a good try with me!'

'Did he?' Sue giggled. 'What happened?'

'He was,' said Paula, thoughtfully, 'a bit over the top, to put it mildly.'

'Paula. . .I think perhaps I should tell you—'

'That you must never judge a book by its cover,' interrupted a deep male voice behind them.

Paula swivelled on the seat and discovered the tall, dark stranger, minus the camera this time, lifting broad shoulders under the denim shirt which tugged at the movement of hard, lazy muscle beneath. An odd little feeling in the pit of her stomach started, the rush she associated with parachute jumps, not that she'd ever made any!

'Oh, Sam, do stop teasing.' Sue hit the tough-looking arm playfully. 'Paula, please meet Dr Sam Carlile, Ken's friend from uni who came to help us out eighteen months ago and stayed much longer than he bargained for. Sam Carlile, meet Paula Harvie, my locum.'

Paula groaned inwardly at her mistake, only comforted by the fact that Sam Carlile seemed just as startled as she. Making an excellent recovery, he tilted his head towards the raucous gathering of children under which

Mrs McDuff was labouring and quirked a dark eyebrow. 'Not a group member, then?'

Paula sat up stiffly. 'You didn't exactly give me the opportunity to introduce myself, Dr Carlile—not with a camera whirring in my face.'

'You seemed to handle the filming well enough.' He allowed his eyes to steal over her as she sat on the seat, taking in the gentle curve of her fair, freshly styled hair and slowly descending over her blue cotton suit jacket which nipped into a small waist.

'Hopefully, you'll be able to edit out my erroneous appearance?' she challenged.

He shrugged dismissively. 'Not unless you want me to.'

Sue seemed to think the situation was highly amusing. 'I can see you two are going to get along famously.' She chuckled. 'Look, I have to get back to Mrs McDuff and lend a hand. Can I leave you safely or should I find someone to referee?'

Sam Carlile shook his head, his eyes not leaving Paula's face. 'Off you go, Sue. . .well be fine. Won't we, Dr Harvie?'

'Absolutely,' echoed Paula, lifting her chin. 'I'm off, anyway. I just wanted you to know I was set for tomorrow, Sue.'

'Dr Dunwoody!' Mrs McDuff's voice contained a note of panic. Reluctantly Sue slipped away.

'Well, well,' Sam Carlile murmured, rocking on his heels.

Paula was uncomfortable under his scrutiny—just as uncomfortable as she had felt under that infuriating lens. What if she hadn't wanted to be filmed? What if she had been obsessively camera-shy and being filmed gave her a rash or red blotches? 'Well, what, Dr Carlile?' She frowned.

'Whoever would have guessed it? That our new

doctor would turn out to be so photogenic.'

'Sorry to disappoint you.' She picked up her bag and smoothed down her suit. 'But as you'll no doubt discover from the film, I'm not in the least photogenic. You took quite a risk, pointing that thing at me. I might have cracked the lens.'

He lifted both eyebrows sharply. 'There's nothing like a sense of humour to get a friendship going, is there?'

'It depends,' Paula retaliated, 'on one's definition of friendship.'

His dark eyes settled on the proud, moist curve of her mouth. 'I thought by the smile you effected so cleverly and instantly for the camera that you may have had lots of practice.'

'At what, for heaven's sake?' Paula would have laughed if she hadn't been so flabbergasted.

He shrugged. 'Being the focus of attention...taking centre stage? Not that it's important...'

'No, it isn't,' she cut in decisively before he got any further. Was it his arrogance that reminded her of Jay? she wondered bitterly. Perhaps she was being premature—but the man to whom she had been married for three years during the early days of her training had left scars deep enough to open at the first hint of male infringement on her private space.

It was strange, this resemblance between the two men. It had nothing to do with the physical—for Jay was blond and blue-eyed and around five feet ten inches in height, whereas this man towered into six feet and his complexion was more Mediterranean than English. The clear comparison between the two men brought a sudden pang of remembrance of Jay and made her wince. She felt stupidly light-headed all of a sudden...

'Are you OK?' Sam Carlile reached out a hand and gently cupped her elbow. 'Look, you'd better sit down.'

Paula felt the heat from his fingers pierce the soft

cotton of her sleeve and quickly she drew her arm away. 'I'm fine, just fine. It's the heat—'

'Or is it the film? If you're so concerned about what you look like, I can always erase it.'

'It's nothing to do with your wretched film,' she protested, reaching for the bench and steadying herself. She was feeling in desperate need of shade from the hot sun and some equally protective shelter from this intrusive stranger.

He held out beautifully shaped hands, darkened at the knuckles by strong sunlight, his short pale nails cut to the firm shape of his fingers. 'Lean on me and I'll walk you to your car because if you faint here you'll have twenty kids trying to give you resuscitation.'

She tried not to look into the dark and oddly disarming brown eyes which seemed to be showing a surprising concern. Worst of all, she did not like the way she responded to that concern. After five long years, could she still feel so wretchedly vulnerable?

Centering her vision determinedly on the house, she took hold of the arm.

'You looked like a frightened rabbit just then,' he announced unhelpfully as they walked across the lawn.

'Thank you,' she muttered helplessly. 'You're doing wonders for the morale.'

'I wouldn't have thought a morale like yours needed boosting.'

'As you yourself said earlier, never judge a book by its cover, Dr Carlile.' She decided she'd rather fall over than be helped any longer, and she pulled away, wondering how the merest flick of fingers across her sleeve could make her feel so disquieted.

He watched her hesitate across the stuffed toys, and when she faltered at the door he lifted deviously tame eyes. 'You're sure you feel up to driving?' he challenged.

'Just as sure as I have been every day for the last fourteen years,' she murmured dryly, and pulled back her shoulders as a soft breeze blew revivingly in through the front door.

'Which makes you roughly thirty. . .thirty-one?' He grinned. 'Old enough to know you shouldn't sit behind a wheel when you're feeling faint.'

Over-conscious of his amused and slightly reproachful eyes on her, she was stunned at the tingle of sensation which rippled through her, annihilating the sense of outrage she should have had at his swift and accurate mathematical reckoning. What on earth was wrong with her?

'You're blushing,' he said with another wide grin. 'Have I touched on a sensitive nerve?'

'My age is of no concern—' she began in a fluster, and then saw by the twinkle in his eyes she had misconstrued his meaning.

'It was the driving bit I was referring to,' he corrected her gently, still with amusement lingering in his tone. 'Go along, then.' He chuckled, shrugging. 'Just be careful.'

Feeling like a dismissed schoolgirl, she hesitated, then turned on her heel and bolted for the car. A block of shops along, she slid the car into the gutter to catch back her breath—and her pounding heart. She felt about as composed as a force-ten gale!

For a moment she sat there, dazed. Sam Carlile had been deadly accurate. Perhaps that was what hurt most of all—her vanity! Yet it had seemed a Godsend when Aunt Steph had written to her and told her that the Dunwoodys were looking for a locum for eight to twelve months. She'd leapt at the chance to retreat from London life precisely because of the kind of superficial socializing that had become a nightmare of late.

Dinner parties had only reminded her of how lonely

she had become and how insular. She had always
planned that by now she would have blended mother-
hood with her skills as a doctor. Perhaps that was why
she'd accepted Jay's excuses all those years ago. And
she'd been blind enough not to see why. . .until her
pregnancy had so painfully enlightened her. Look at
Sue Dunwoody, she taunted herself. A Down's child, a
practice and a pregnancy—and still able to cope.

What hand of fate had made it so impossible for her
to achieve her own dreams? She was a traditionalist at
heart, wasn't she? Marriage was the natural outcome of
falling in love, and she had believed Jay felt the same.
Perhaps at twenty-three she had had no conception of
what it would be like trying to divide herself between
a husband and training—but Jay had simply swept her
off her feet. Perhaps he too had been caught up in a
fantasy. A fantasy that had suddenly become a terrifying
reality when Emily had been born two months prematurely.

Paula flipped on a cassette, resolutely started the car
and, as she drove the fifteen minute journey to Warwick,
wondered if she was right in moving to Struan. It made
no odds to her career, leaving the city. Struan was just
a stepping stone, coincidental to her plans, but Sam
Carlile had taken the wind out of her sails. She tried to
concentrate on the lovely countryside, the quaint village
pubs with leaning walls, and narrow, leafy roads. But
by the time she arrived at the castle and passed by its
grey stone walls, driving slowly into Marble Lane, she
had almost decided to phone Sue and tell her it had been
a mistake.

However, Aunt Steph would hear none of it. 'He's a
sweetie underneath,' she said of Sam Carlile as they ate
Sunday afternoon tea on the lawn. 'Once you get to
know him, you'll revise your opinion, Paula. Besides
which, he isn't staying—you do know that, don't you?'

'No, I didn't,' Paula admitted, feeling greatly relieved.

'He's going back to Delhi,' her aunt replied with a sigh. 'More's the pity.'

'Delhi as in India?' queried Paula uncertainly.

'Yes. He came back to England when the funds ran out for the specialist hospital unit he had started. He's waiting to hear if some sponsoring he's been trying to drum up over the last eighteen months has come through. So maybe you won't be bothered by him for too long, dear. Although, as far as his patients go, they won't find another Sam Carlile again, that's for sure.'

Paula was inclined to agree, but not in the sense her aunt meant. She leaned back in the recliner pensively. He was the type of character she would find hard to work with—to be specific, she told herself firmly, the kind of man she wanted to avoid. Well, after today, perhaps he was just as eager to avoid her.

'Have another pastry, Paula,' her aunt tempted her, and, feeling better, Paula took one and slid it onto her plate. 'He was romantically involved with a female doctor in India,' her aunt added casually, 'but it all fizzled out.'

'Poor woman,' muttered Paula wryly. 'Why is it I'm not surprised?'

Her aunt sighed. 'Just you look into his eyes next time, dear. That man's been wounded.'

Wounded my foot, Paula thought, munching hard on her pastry. It would take a pretty impressive weapon to penetrate that thickness of skin. Still, she wasn't going to argue with her aunt—Sam Carlile had caused enough commotion for one day.

As they sat companionably together Paula studied the kind and gentle but rather naive lines of her aunt's face. Whatever would she have done without Aunt Steph in her life?

For after her mother's death, when Paula had been

little more than eight, Aunt Steph, her mother's sister, had adopted her. Her wandering reprobate of a father had, of course, been nowhere to be found. He'd left her mother just after Paula's birth, flown to Australia to seek his fortune and not returned, apart from one or two fleeting visits, before his death in a mining accident.

And now dear Aunt Steph, who had moved from North London to Warwick after she'd retired, had alerted her to the vacancy arising for a locum doctor at Struan House Surgery.

As for Sue, Paula had liked her immediately. Sue had explained that she and her husband Ken were aiming to develop the five-thousand patient practice. John Linton, originally their locum, was interested in a partnership—but other than that, Paula knew relatively little of the politics of a country practice.

'Sam and Kenneth Dunwoody are buddies, you see, from university,' her aunt was saying. 'When the Dunwoodys took on this practice they tried to twist Sam's arm to go into partnership with them. But he's set on India.'

'Suddenly I'm grateful to India!' Paula commented wryly.

The older woman chuckled. 'Oh, his banter is just a bluff. When he tried to boss me around I told him I was far too long in the tooth to be organized by a whipper-snapper like him.'

Paula giggled. 'What did he say?'

'He laughed and said I reminded him of Barbara Stanwyck, his favourite black-and-white-movie actress who was supposed to breathe fire at her leading men.'

Paula snorted. 'Well, lucky you, Aunt Steph. I wasn't singled out for such special treatment.'

'That's because you're young and beautiful,' her aunt smiled. 'I'm old enough to flatter quite safely.'

Paula drank her tea, wondering if she had weighed

up Sam Carlile entirely correctly. Could her first impressions towards him have clouded her judgement? Perhaps there was more to the man than she thought, though, quite frankly, she reminded herself as she caught Aunt Steph's interested blue eyes, she had no intention of finding out.

She'd taken on the locum job as a precursor to discovering just what kind of practice she wanted for her future. She wasn't going to let a perfect stranger upset her plans. Everything else was wonderful about Struan House Surgery. She was sure she could manage Sam Carlile.

He simply needed ignoring, that was all.

CHAPTER TWO

STRUAN HOUSE SURGERY sheltered comfortably under the weight of Georgian beams. It had once been, so Paula discovered, a hostelry, its stables now converted into treatment rooms—thanks to an enterprising GP in the seventies who had moved in and refurbished it as a practice. It nevertheless looked perfectly right, sitting in between the Beeswax Hotel and a Victorian forge which was now a small library. Five minutes along the road was Struan high street, a busy market centre and, at the weekend, a fisherman's paradise.

Paula parked her car in the tiny green square opposite the surgery on Monday morning, sniffing the fresh, clear air as she stretched and cast her eyes along the road. She could hardly believe she was in the twentieth century, and if it hadn't been for the stallholders setting up their wares, she thought, she could probably have been stepping into a scene from Dickens. It was a comfortable feeling. Different indeed to north London and the busy practice of eight doctors in a bustling health centre where she had spent the last five years.

Just then a horn tooted and a grey car purred up beside her. Her heart sank. She'd been hoping to arrive at surgery before anyone else, it was five to eight and the surgeries didn't begin until half past. But, lo and behold, Sam Carlile jumped out of the car and came around to meet her.

He looked distinctive, and for a moment she could imagine him in Delhi, not in the informal short-sleeved shirt and linen trousers he was wearing today, but wearing a white coat and issuing orders to the nursing staff

18

of the hospital, who doubtless worshipped the ground he trod on. Well, she wasn't one of them, thank God!

'Hi!' she greeted him nonchalantly, tugging her case from the Polo without looking at him, telling herself she wasn't all fingers and thumbs—even if she had dropped her keys behind the seat into an annoying little crevice.

'Hi, yourself.' He stood watching her, his eyes amused as she fought to capture them. 'Are we on speaking terms today?'

When she eventually emerged from behind the seat she smiled, attempting to thrust her hair from her face in a graceful gesture as well as locking the car at the same time. 'I'm sorry?' She shot him a puzzled expression, though she knew what he was talking about.

'I think we might have got off on the wrong foot— Paula.' He grinned.

She shrugged. 'Not at all—Sam.'

'Well—I'm relieved.' He began to walk across the narrow road with her, his long legs moving one stride to her two. 'Oh, by the way, I'm next door if you want me today. If there's anything you need help with.'

'I'm sure I won't need to disturb you—but thank you all the same.'

'Like that, is it?' He chuckled as he pushed open the surgery door for her. 'A lady of independence.'

She shot him a puzzled look. 'No, it's just that I know my job, that's all.'

'Ah!' He tutted. 'A career woman.'

'You sound prejudiced, Sam,' she answered equably—not that she felt equable, but she wasn't going to let him under her skin this morning. 'What a pity. I had taken you for a broader-thinking man.'

'I was once,' he retorted with a trace of rare cynicism in his tone. 'But I seem to have come across too many career women to allow my thinking to get much broader.'

She lifted her eyebrows. 'Really? And you propose to judge me on previous experience?'

'Experience—and lessons learnt,' he told her cryptically.

She smiled brightly and waved at the girls in Reception, smothering both her curiosity and anger. Surely his kind of attitude had gone out with the ark? But then, she had detected another note in his voice, something a little more personal—and a little more disquieting.

'I'm glad to see our reception staff deserve such an effusive welcome,' he said caustically.

'They are, it seems,' Paula returned sweetly, 'genuinely pleased to see me!' She had a feeling as she talked to Bella Poole and Tricia Wakefield—both in their mid-thirties—that someone's eyes were burning into her shoulders, but she avoided looking and was grateful the cleaning lady's vacuum cleaner buzzed loudly enough to cause a distraction.

After chatting for a few moments, she walked along the narrow corridor, past the treatment rooms. The corridor had beams and roughened white plaster walls, and at the end of it she turned into the consulting room which was to be hers and sat down at her desk, taking a moment or two to drink in her surroundings.

It was a small, pleasantly whitewashed room with a great oak lintel across the door; there was a scalloped blind in ivory, deep red carpeting and a comfortable examination bench—Yes, she could be happy here.

'May I come in?' Sam Carlile poked his dark head around the door and instantly dispelled the prospect of happiness. One black eyebrow arched curiously at the computer. 'Need any help deciphering this?' He clucked his tongue, lifting his eyes to the ceiling. 'Now what an absurd question to put to such an experienced lady!'

Paula sat in her seat and smiled sweetly. 'I've the general gist, thanks very much.'

'Struan's rather a change from London, isn't it?' he went on, undaunted. 'One extreme to another? What could Struan possibly offer a woman like you? Not running away from anything—or anyone—by any chance?'

She gave a short laugh. 'I beg your pardon?'

He shrugged. 'You're single—so Sue tells me. You're plainly confident—the kind of woman who knows where she's going in life. Where does a dull little place like Struan fit, in the scheme of your grand plan?'

Paula snorted. 'Are you always so damned objectionable first thing in the morning?'

'Objectionable?' He grinned. 'Am I?'

'Look, Sam—'

'I am looking,' he said drolly, casting his eyes over her. 'And I can see in a glance you've made yourself at home.'

'Despite your warm welcome!'

'It's just that I'm not totally convinced that working in a rural practice like this is really your thing.'

'My thing!' she gasped affronted. 'I might very well make the same observation of you. I understand you'd given your undivided attention to the Third World as recently as eighteen months ago. Struan can hardly hold much of a challenge for one so intensely committed to saving mankind.'

He held up his hands in mock surrender. '*Touché*—for the moment. But don't forget, I'm just next door in case of a dire emergency—like one of the Beeswax mice scurrying across the floor. Occasionally they lose their flight path home, you know.'

'Mice?' she stammered as he opened the door. 'Real mice?'

'They don't bite,' he called from the corridor. 'Not usually.'

The door clinked shut. She gazed furtively around the wainscoting, a shiver going down her spine. Mice. What rubbish. Trust a man to have the last word. She glared at the door, trying to analyze why the shiver should seem to bear more relation to the drift of aftershave lingering in the room than the prospect of mice.

How did he manage to guess so accurately about her? She was professionally confident and reasonably ambitious. But that was because, despite Jay's affair and the loss of Emily, she had completed her training, found a place with the North London practice and successfully juggled just about every equation of patient problem that had been hurled her way. Perhaps she had become insular and independent—even solitary, sometimes—but she had coped with her grief, held herself together.

'Hi, Paula! How's it going?' Sue Dunwoody appeared at the open door. With her was a fair-haired young man and an older man of around forty carrying a slight paunch.

Ken Dunwoody strode in and shook her hand firmly. 'I'm Sue's partner in crime, and this is John Linton. Sorry we couldn't meet a couple of weeks back—I was on call, I'm afraid, and John here was feeding his face as usual in Warwick. Lucky devil.'

John made a few disparaging remarks in Ken's direction as the practice nurse, Julia Goodman, joined them. After a few minutes of conversation the little crowd broke up to go to their respective surgeries, and, pushing Sam Carlile firmly to the back of her mind, Paula began to meet some of the inhabitants of Struan and Warwick.

One of these was Sally Walker, a vivacious blonde of thirty-six who, after a number of miscarriages, was fourteen weeks pregnant.

'Immunotherapy helped eventually,' Sally told her as Paula wrapped the rubbery cuff around her arm and checked her blood pressure. 'Selwyn and I tried for a family for about five years, then Dr Carlile fixed us up with an appointment at a clinic in London. As you can see it worked. But recently I've had indigestion. It woke me in the night. I had to get up, and I suppose I started to worry.'

Paula nodded, helping her to the couch. 'Who do you normally see?'

'Dr Carlile. But when I heard there was another lady doctor I asked if I could see you. It's rather nice to have a full-time lady doctor available. Dr Dunwoody is part time now she's pregnant, isn't she?'

Paula nodded. 'Yes. . .that's why I'm here. In a while, she'll cut down to one day a week for her antenatal clinic only.'

Sally was concerned with the area of discomfort across her back. It was hard to decipher whether there was a muscular problem since she presented mixed symptoms which were often temporary and fluid.

'Everything all right?' Sally asked as she slid down from the couch.

'Yes, absolutely.' Paula gestured to her to sit down again. 'Apart from the indigestion and the shoulder, is there anything else troubling you?'

Sally shrugged. 'A little tired, a bit sick and dizzy. But am I imagining these things, I wonder? The miscarriages have made me paranoid. Selwyn says I should try to de-stress somehow.'

'Do you feel under any particular stress—apart from the pregnancy?'

Sally sighed. 'Not really. I'm just terrified it's not going to work out. I try to do my yoga and breathing, but it seems a vicious circle. Sometimes my heart seems to falter, palpitate with apprehension, if you know what I mean. Selwyn says I'm a born worrier.'

Paula smiled kindly. 'I think he's probably right about worry—it doesn't help, but then trying not to worry sometimes sets up an adverse reaction. Do these palpitations only occur when you find yourself worrying?'

Sally frowned. 'I suppose so.' She sighed. 'I try to ignore them.'

Paula hesitated, instinct telling her that something was not as it should be, though she could find nothing physically wrong with Sally to suggest a problem. All the same, she was concerned. 'I'd like you to pop along a little earlier to the hospital,' she told Sally as she studied the details given on the computer and saw Sally's appointment for a fortnight away. 'Just to be on the safe side, that's all. At least your consultant will be able to put your mind at rest.'

Sally nodded slowly. 'If you think it's best.' She hesitated, blushing under her fair skin. 'To be truthful, I hate hospitals. Every time I go there I feel legless.'

'They're not much fun, are they?' Paula hesitated as her hand went to the phone. 'But where would we be without them?'

'It's really necessary—do you think?' Sally protested, biting her lip.

Paula pressed the internal buzzer. 'Tell you what, I'll speak to Dr Carlile and see if he can come in for a minute or two. That will ease both our minds.'

But Sam had been called away on an emergency. Paula didn't want to create a sense of urgency with Sally, yet she felt she should not lose time in having Sally seen. She made her decision, and, after telling Sally to go home and make herself a cup of tea and put her feet up, she phoned the hospital in Warwick and spoke to Peter Reed who was managing the pregnancy.

She found him an approachable paediatrician and explained her concerns, and he promised to have his secretary contact Sally. After this, Paula's morning progressed well, with most of Sue's transferred patients happy to see her.

At lunch time she went with John Linton to the Beeswax and ordered coffee and sandwiches. He was married to a solicitor, she discovered, and they lived in Warwick. It was understood that when Sam returned to Delhi, John would take on a partnership with the Dunwoodys.

Unlike Sam, he asked her no searching questions and she found herself in a relaxed frame of mind when she began afternoon surgery again. Sam reappeared at the end of the day when he bumped into her by the cars, though whether by luck or judgement she wasn't sure.

The sun was low in the April sky, spreading a soft golden glow across the horizon, and the birds were singing, perched on the silver branches of the trees on the green. He leaned against the bonnet of the Polo whilst she unlocked it, and lifted his wrist to study his watch.

'We've time for a quick half at the Beeswax, if you like,' he said, without much enthusiasm as far as Paula could interpret. As a welcoming gesture, the offer held about as much warmth as a freezer. Paula opened the car door and pushed in her bags. 'No, thanks,' she called over her shoulder. 'I'm sure you're far too exhausted to have to think up polite conversation. I know I certainly am.'

'I couldn't make it at lunch time, I'm afraid. Sue asked me if I'd see how you were—she didn't like to think of you eating alone.'

'Well, I'm sorry to disappoint you,' Paula muttered as she drew herself upright, 'But I've had lunch. In the Beeswax, with John. The coffee and company were excellent.'

He frowned at her. 'Somehow I feel a little rejected.'

'You? You feel rejected?'

He looked vague. 'Have I said something to upset you?'

Paula shook her head in amazement. 'Nothing I won't recover from, I don't suppose.'

If she was prepared to stand here and argue with him,

Paula told herself, then she was a fool, because she knew exactly what this man was made of. She had had three solid years of practice with Jay, and, if that didn't qualify her to recognize the signs of male ego, she didn't know what did.

How in heaven's name Sam Carlile managed general practice in a small town—with ordinary, everyday people—she had no idea. Perhaps that was why he was back off to Delhi again in his principal role as saviour-doctor to the Third World, where he would doubtless receive all the adulation he so obviously thrived on— but which he certainly wasn't about to receive from her.

'I'm sorry, but I'm late,' she said tersely, and she jumped into the Polo, unintentionally showing a long expanse of leg as her skirt rode up. The movement had not been missed.

She snatched down her hem and fumbled the door closed, starting the car with a thrust of accelerator and reversing into the street. It was only when she had arrived in Warwick and was turning into Marble Lane that she realized she had forgotten to mention Sally Walker, which was intensely annoying because Sally was his patient and the only one she had seen during the day who had not transferred from Sue. The man had distracted her to such a point, she'd forgotten completely.

As she wandered into Aunt Steph's pretty flower-filled garden which led to her flat, she wondered if she should ring him back. But then, it would seem as if she was using Sally as an excuse to prolong the argument— which she wasn't. It could wait until next time she saw him, she supposed, but, even so, it was vexing.

As it happened, tomorrow never came. Or at least it came and went without Paula seeing Sam Carlile. Perhaps for an instant she spotted him at lunch time, zooming off in the Mercedes. But for the rest of the day she was out on calls and absorbed in working out the unfamiliar geography of the village which, in fact, was far more extensive than she had imagined.

However, most of her calls were for minor complaints; one was to six year-old Jamie Lawrence who had just recovered from a bout of chickenpox. Paula sipped the cup of tea Mrs Lawrence had made aware that Jamie had not stopped hopping and skipping about the room for the full ten minutes she had been there.

'He's wearing me out,' complained Mrs Lawrence as her son catapulted himself into the garden. 'He doesn't sleep but a few hours. I thought the chickenpox would tire him out like other kids. His brothers and sister all sat up on the couch when they had it, watching TV. Not Jamie, though. Can I send him back to school do you think?'

Paula glanced at the boy's notes. 'I see he has been taking Phenergan to relieve his sneezing bouts—you've had several repeat prescriptions?'

Mrs Lawrence carried on making the family's tea. Bread and peanut butter sandwiches, crisps and a bottle of fizzy drink stood on the kitchen table. 'Oh, the allergy's cleared up, whatever it was! The thing is, he doesn't sneeze now, but Phenergan seems to settle him at night.'

Paula stood up and watched Jamie in the garden kicking a bucket around. 'Is he ever irritable?' she asked.

'Who, Jamie?' Mrs Lawrence chuckled. 'He's a bad-tempered little snake all right. We put it down to him being hyperactive. Anyway, have I got the all clear to send him to school next week?'

Paula nodded. 'I've checked him over. He's fine physically. He can go to school.'

'Thank the Lord for that.' Mrs Lawrence

accompanied her to the door. 'Can I have some more of that Phenergan?'

'You know, if Jamie's allergy has cleared for the moment, I think we could try to investigate his hyperactivity from a different angle,' Paula suggested. 'Could you come in to see me when you've a moment or two spare?'

Mrs Lawrence shrugged. 'I suppose so. Can't think what you can do about Jamie's ups and downs, though. He needs his sleep—and so do I!'

Paula smiled. 'Well, there must be something. Let's put our heads together, shall we?'

The next day, Wednesday, Paula assisted Sue with the antenatal clinic. Paula weighed and took blood pressure and familiarized herself with the pregnant mums. Karen Shore and Brenda Vance were due in a few days, and both were booked into Warwick maternity as firsttime mums. Sally Walker did not turn up, which Sue remarked on, but Paula imagined that she had attended the appointment she'd made with the consultant. Jane Brookes and Joanne Namu were nineteen and twenty respectively and in their fourth months of pregnancy, and Kylie Grant was expecting twins.

'Quite a mixed bag,' Sue commented as she discussed the notes with Paula afterwards. 'When I'm not around, do you think you'll cope?'

Paula laughed softly. 'Just about, I should think. Jane and Joanne are presenting no special problems, and Karen and Brenda are both due shortly. Kylie, too. It really only leaves me with Sally Walker and new additions.'

Sue nodded thoughtfully. 'Sally was originally Sam's patient. Is he not seeing her?'

Paula shrugged. 'I'm not sure.' She explained that Sally had been in to see her and what had happened. 'I should have mentioned it to Sam, I suppose. Trouble is, there was nothing specific I could find—just a hunch.'

Sue grinned. 'Better than anything, hunches of that sort. Still, perhaps it would be wise to mention it to Sam.'

Paula nodded. 'I'll try to flag him down today.'

But, though she tried to catch him at five, he had gone, and the following day was his day off. So when Friday came she was surprised to find a memo on her desk from Sam, asking for 'an audience' later that day.

Mrs Lawrence called to see her during the morning. 'Jamie's back at school,' she told Paula. 'Let's hope that takes the stuffing out of him. I wish there were pills I could give him to calm him.'

'Not a good idea,' Paula countered swiftly, although the suggestion had come in joke form. 'Treatment for hyperactivity is usually more likely to include talking to the rest of the family, his teachers, support groups and sometimes psychiatrists.'

'Well,' said Mrs Lawrence firmly, 'we've had four kids to bring up, and I can tell you it hasn't been easy, but they've all been fed and clothed and cared for. And, I might add, Len and I are still together, which is more than I can say for some of the families at his school.'

Paula nodded. 'You've done extremely well,' she said encouragingly. 'I imagine it's not easy with a young family—which is why I'd like to try to help you with Jamie's ongoing problem.'

The woman was thoughtful. 'I appreciate the offer. But what can I do? Phenergan has been the only answer.'

'I was wondering if Jamie does much sport?' Paula enquired.

'I wish he did,' his mum sighed. 'But he won't be part of a team. He's such an individualist.'

'What about swimming?'

'It's the money, isn't it? Costs a fortune, going to the

baths these days. And he has to travel to Warwick; there's nothing in Struan.'

'A club?' Paula mused. 'Surely there's a group or club in Struan who share expenses?'

Mrs Lawrence shrugged. 'I don't know. There's a gap of five years between Jamie and his next sister. The other children were all involved with school sports anyway.'

Paula hesitated. 'There's one more thing. There is new research—quite exciting new research—to suggest there is a link between hyperactivity and essential fatty acids.'

'And what are they when they're at home, for heaven's sake?' gasped Mrs Lawrence.

'Essential fatty acids are the equivalent of vitamins and play an important role in the manufacture of hormones. Plus they're building blocks for cell walls throughout the body. You get them in food like oily fish, nuts and leafy green vegetables, but not, I'm afraid, in things like fizzy drinks or crisps.'

Mrs Lawrence lifted an eyebrow. 'Oh, dear.'

Paula smiled. 'If you like I can give you an address and telephone number of a support group who will tell you very much more than I can. The founder members were the first to identify the fatty acid link with hyperactivity. I'm sure you'll find them helpful.'

Mrs Lawrence considered the suggestion. 'Well, perhaps I'll think about it.'

When Mrs Lawrence left, Paula contemplated the case thoughtfully. She would have to see if the idea was attractive enough to start Jamie's mum on some research.

It was quite late in the day when Paula finally got around to meeting Sam after surgery. He stopped her in the hall just as Julia Goodman, the practice nurse, passed them *en route* to her room.

'You wanted to talk to me?' Paula made it plain she

was on her way out, with her bag over her shoulder and case in hand.

'I most certainly do.'

'Where?' She pushed back a silky blonde lock of hair from her grey eyes. 'My room or yours?'

He took her elbow and propelled her along the corridor. 'Let's talk outside in the sunshine, shall we?'

Once outside, he turned to face her. 'I didn't want to talk in there. Not with staff still around.'

'The walls seem pretty thick to me.' She frowned. 'Do I take it I've done something wrong?'

'Nothing that you won't have an eminently good excuse for, I'm sure.'

Just then, John Linton came up. 'Hi, you two. Drink at the Beeswax before you disappear?'

'Ah. . .no, thanks, John,' Sam declined. 'Catch you later, perhaps.'

Paula felt sorry for him. 'Perhaps a sandwich at lunch time tomorrow, John?'

'Great.' He propelled himself towards his car. 'See you then.'

Sam looked at her sharply. 'I shouldn't encourage that if I were you.'

'Encourage what, for goodness' sake?'

'Lunch hours at the Beeswax.'

'John,' she gasped, 'was kind enough to show me a little welcoming spirit when everyone else was too busy.'

'You didn't ask me.'

'I shouldn't have needed to. Besides, I wouldn't have thought you would want to waste a valuable lunch time in the presence of a hard-hearted career woman.'

'I told you, it was nothing personal.'

She stared at him imcredulously. 'Sam—I can't believe we're having this conversation.'

'Well, then, let's talk about something else. Sally Walker for example.'

Paula groaned inwardly. She had forgotten Sally. Almost before she could begin to explain a woman came running up to Sam, beginning to itemize a list of health hiccups. He was patient enough, Paula noticed. Only the slight flush creeping up his neck under the deep tan gave any clue as to the impatience he was feeling.

Eventually, after persuading the woman to make an appointment, he turned back to Paula, running a hand through the mass of jet-black hair. 'Look, I don't want to pick an argument, but Sally is my patient. I think we need to talk.'

Paula hesitated for a moment but then shrugged. She'd much rather get this thing over and done with tonight, not have it looming over the weekend, and she was, technically, in the wrong. 'Where do you suggest we go?' she asked finally.

'What about an hour's fresh air? Do you know the Shallows?'

'I've a map—'

'You'll never find it in a million years.' He fished in his pocket for his keys. 'Come on, we'll take the Mercedes.' At Paula's silent refusal to budge he gave a short laugh. 'Afraid?' he challenged softly. 'Afraid you won't be able to run off when the going gets tough?'

I've never run away yet, Sam—from anything,' she retorted, turning on her heel and marching towards the grey car.

Soon she found herself in the front seat of the Mercedes, beside a man whom she now knew enough about to know she was on very dangerous territory, and had probably been provoked into coming along to the Shallows so that he could tear her to verbal shreds.

As he drove she found her eyes slipping to the deeply tanned arms beside her. Every so often, her gaze dropped to the long legs encased in dark cotton, so long they seemed never ending, and every now and then as he changed gear solid thigh muscle rose and fell rhythmically.

The screech of a bird made her jump, and her gaze jerked up to the windscreen. The winding lane had evolved into a slope towards the water, and a slip of glittering grey water gleamed in the evening sun. 'I thought this place might have a calming effect,' he muttered dryly. 'On both of us.'

'Or either one of us can jump in to cool off,' she parried, glancing at him under lowered lids.

'Perhaps that's not such a bad suggestion.' He smiled, quirking an eyebrow. 'Ever been skinny-dipping?'

For a moment she thought he was serious. 'Years ago,' she confessed, 'when I was a kid.' She held out a hand, a teasing light in her eye. 'Feel free to go ahead. I'll watch and make sure you're not disturbed.'

He laughed, bringing the car to a halt. 'I believe you would as well.'

Torn between confusion and a hot warmth that seemed to be seeping up from her toes, she closed her mouth and reluctantly let her eyes linger on the pale grey sheet of river and willowy trees bathed in a fine, shimmering mist of evening. Trying not to think of Sam Carlile without a shred of clothing took more self-control than she'd bargained for.

To compose herself she climbed out of the car and took a deep breath of air. The ground beneath her feet was dry and gently sloping, and the air embalmed her like silk.

'This way,' he called, beckoning her. 'Watch out for mini-estuaries.' He held out his hand as she came towards him. There was a gap of several feet filled with sludgy water across which she must jump. 'Here. . .' he held out a hand. . .'I'll catch you. Those crazy things you have on your feet look like death traps.'

She gave him a withering look but, realizing he was right and she might just fall in her heels and look even more of an idiot, she took the offered hand and tried not to acknowledge the instant shock wave of his fingers sending a spiral of sensation along her arm.

'OK, jump!' he called, lifting provocative brown eyes. 'If you dare.'

She dared. He caught her firmly, as promised, by the waist and drew her to him. They stood rockily together for a second, her breath catching in her throat at the close physical contact, her heart lurching crazily as he steadied them.

'You're safe,' he told her with an amused grin, his breath stroking her face as his brown eyes danced teasingly above her. With a start she discovered she was leaning pleasurably into the curve of his strong body, her hands on his shoulders and her cotton dress curved to the line of his body.

'Th. . .thanks. . .' she managed, exerting what control she had left over her traitorous body, ashamed of the crack in her voice as she spoke.

Better hang on, though,' he warned her, offering his hand once more. 'There are a few more ahead.'

I think I'll just about manage,' she informed him, and, walking determinedly on along the river bank, she smoothed down her dress with shaky hands.

'I. . .I'm sorry about Sally,' she said as he caught up with her, hoping her inner confusion was only apparent to herself. 'I should have told you. . .or at least left you a note. I had every intention—'

'Good intention didn't help much when Peter phoned me and I hadn't the least idea what he was talking about.'

Her heart sank. 'What happened when he saw Sally?'

He was silent, walking beside her, catching up a reed every so often to stroke between his fingers. 'He checked her thoroughly and the baby's fine. He seems certain there should be no reason to doubt this will be a full-term pregnancy.'

Paula nodded slowly. 'Because of the success of the immunotherapy?'

He shrugged. 'Who can say? I would have liked to see Sally myself that day and arrived at my own conclusions.'

'Didn't the girls at Reception tell you? I held on to her for a while, hoping you'd return from your emergency, but I couldn't string it out any longer. She's a worrier, and her history—'

'Is one of the reasons I needed to be told.'

'I did the next best thing.'

'And then clearly forgot all about it. You must have been concerned over Sally to have phoned Peter. Heaven, woman, how did it escape your memory? Or was it a case of deliberate forgetfulness?'

'That's absurd,' Paula protested, coming to an abrupt halt. 'Why should I deliberately not tell you?'

'Because you felt it wasn't necessary, presumably. Because you felt confident enough with your own judgement, despite the fact she is my patient?'

'Now I know it's not my imagination.' Paula gasped in dismay. 'You do resent me.'

'Resent you?' His face darkened and he drew in his lips. 'No, I don't resent you personally. But I do resent professionals in general who imagine they are a law unto themselves and refuse to work within a team.'

'Don't you mean women professionals?' Paula's voice all but deserted her. 'Would you still be having this conversation if I were a man?'

They faced each other in silence and Paula waited for the eruption. She was treading on eggshells already over Sally, and she would probably have fared better by keeping quiet, but she had the unnerving feeling that Sam Carlile resented more than just the fact she had forgotten to mention Sally. As it was, he dug his hands deeply in his pockets and turned to stare out over the shimmering grey water.

After a few moments Paula took a breath. 'I'm sorry,' she sighed. 'I shouldn't have said that. But I'm afraid I feel your dislike of me quite deeply.'

He quirked an eyebrow as he glanced back at her. 'Can you bring yourself to tell this misogynist exactly why you rang a consultant over his head?'

Paula bit her lip. 'I can try. Though the bottom line is, it was purely a very strong feeling that something was not right.' Paula hesitated, wondering if she should voice her thoughts. 'To be honest, I thought if we weren't sidetracked by the pregnancy—the cardiovascular system might be worth checking out. The indigestion and palpitations worried me.'

He frowned. 'Sally's no history of a heart problem. Did you mention it to Peter?'

She shrugged. 'I thought he wouldn't want someone—a locum—coming on heavily with theories. I have little understanding of her case history other than what I saw on her records, and haven't been here two minutes to make a diagnosis.'

'But you don't mind upsetting me?'

She smiled weakly. 'I had upset you, anyway.'

He sighed, shaking his head, bringing up his eyes to meet hers. 'Well, now she appears to be half your patient and half mine. What do you propose doing if she consults you again? Call her in for bed rest?'

'She isn't my patient at all,' Paula protested. 'But if she were I'd have to think carefully about it. Sally mentioned she dislikes hospitals. It could have an adverse effect—you know, hospital aversion and long days of inertia...causing an anxiety syndrome. And, anyway, I'm probably way off-beam on the angina.'

'Or maybe not. Maybe it could be the safest thing all round to have her in.'

She found herself gazing into deep, deep brown eyes which seemed to have the entire spring evening reflected in them. She steeled herself to resist their pull, aware of quivering sensation infiltrating her skin, and it took all her resolve to ignore the tiny darts of flame over her body as she found herself unable to move. What was it in those expressive eyes that Aunt Steph had said had been wounded?

Almost at once the answer came back—it must have been a certain type of woman who had hurt him so deeply. Her gaze slipped involuntarily to his lips, to the generously curved outline and the white slash of teeth, which made the tiny hairs rise on the back of her neck and her body tremble in the soft evening breeze.

Suddenly the screech of an owl shattered the silence and Paula turned involuntarily to gaze over the translucent water. 'It's very beautiful here.' She sighed. 'Does the path go much further?'

'Oh, a fair bit. The river winds down to several estuaries, the Nene to the Wash and the Cherwell to the Thames. Then there's the lovely Leam—she swells on a twenty-five-mile course to the Avon. A good proportion of the river finally goes out into the Bristol Channel.'

He stopped and lifted a hand to shade his face against the crimson glare of the setting sun, the dark irises of his eyes glinting with the sensual combination of sun on water. 'Funny, isn't it? Just like our hundreds of blood vessels and arteries, all flowing conscientiously along as the poor old heart works like thunder to pump life around its very complacent owner—until something goes wrong and we wonder why it has. Pollution, blockage, stress, drought—what applies to our beautiful world applies to us, and yet do we ever link the two and take heed?'

As she watched him, Paula found she was transfixed by the depth of energy in his voice, the quiet passion. For a moment she felt she had glimpsed the flip side of a man who confounded and disturbed her in a far more provocative sense than when he was intent on upsetting her.

He looked slowly back to meet her gaze. His eyes were full of intensity and his smile was warm and wonderful as it melted across her. She was drawn to him against her will, her heart missing a beat as she told herself not to look into his eyes. But the temptation was too great and she gave herself up to the desire to look wondering why she was allowing herself to submit to the sudden and shocking arousal of her newly awakened emotions towards him.

'It. . .is a little chilly,' she stammered, and began to hug herself, aware he had taken off his jacket and was draping it around her shoulders.

'Warmer?' he whispered, lifting her hair with his fingers and trailing it softly over the collar.

She nodded, swallowing, weakened by the sensation of his fingers and his expression.

'Come on,' he said, and took her hand as the mist curled around their ankles until there was nothing left to be seen of the countryside.

CHAPTER THREE

As the days passed, Paula discovered there was only one way to handle Sam Carlile. The technique consisted of, quite simply, giving as good as she got. If he requested a response from her, she gave one without even so much as a second's hesitation, keeping her manner cool and clinical.

She slipped up a couple of times—times painful enough to remember with dismay. The first was a misguided discussion about gender and the workplace which almost ended in violence, simply because he took the hypothesis to the limit, suggesting that marriage to professional women suffered in ninety-nine per cent of cases because women had distanced themselves from the home, putting family life a poor second to ambition and career. She told him he was spouting absolute rubbish.

The second mistake was the result of staying too late and alone at the surgery. And she was tired.

There was a case she was battling with, that of a certain Harry Bamford, who was pressing for an osteotomy, an operation to correct ankylosing spondylitus, the inflammation of joints linking the vertebrae. The error was in asking Sam for help!

He had no intention of ever seriously helping her, she realized. And she felt that if he had not been away from the practice at her interview he would have put up quite a fight over Sue's decision to employ her. She wouldn't make the mistake of asking for his help again.

As Paula drove to work, several days later, she was rehearsing her next interview with Mr Bamford, thinking how she might approach his massive obesity problem from a new angle.

Her first two patients presented minor illnesses, flu and an ear syringing which she gave to the practice nurse, and the third, disconcertingly, was Harry Bamford.

'Have you thought about the operation I asked for?' he asked as soon as he came in and squeezed himself into the patient's chair. He was a heavy-jowelled man, quite grossly overweight, and he moved with increasing difficulty. He looked sixty, though he was barely forty.

'How is the new exercise routine coming along?' Paula countered firmly, wondering if he had kept to any of the exercises the hospital physio had prescribed for him.

'Oh, fine,' he lied audaciously. 'But it doesn't do me any good. I only have to look at food and the weight goes on. I'm sure if I had one of these ops that I read about my backache would go and then I'd lose weight.'

Paula shook her head. 'It's the other way around, I'm afraid. You need to lose weight for an operation. An osteotomy is a surgical procedure used for straightening out bent or fused bones and it often puts the spinal cord at risk. I can't see the sense of risking this when losing weight would be the first step to helping the problem. Invasive techniques aren't to be taken lightly—'

'Nor is chronic backache and painful hips,' interrupted Harry miserably. 'I'm in agony all the time and I'm eating those pills like sweets.'

Paula studied her computer screen, dismayed to think she seemed to be losing the battle with her patient. He had seemed so receptive to her initial suggestions when she'd first come to the surgery. 'How is the slimming class?' she asked cautiously.

'They've given me up, I think.'

'Or you've given them up?'

Harry shrugged. 'I'll never lose weight.'

'Look, let's have one more try.'

'It won't work, Doc. I've been fat and ugly all my life.'

'Rubbish,' Paula dismissed. 'You could be thinner and fitter if you really wanted—try the slimming club once more, will you?'

Harry sighed and wheezed—another sign of his condition worsening, she thought. The ribs could become involved to the point where they joined the spine, so reducing Harry's ability to breathe because of constriction of the lungs. Chest infection would then be an ever-present possibility.

'All right, Doc. If you insist. But I'm only doing it for you.'

Which was a pity, thought Paula, because if he was making the effort for himself he'd probably have a great deal more success. As it was, he seemed to have lost his self-esteem.

It was just after this that Sam knocked on her door.

'Good morning. What a surprise,' she said coolly.

Without preamble he lowered himself into the seat Harry had just vacated. 'I'm taking Poppy out to choose a puppy on Saturday,' he said, and waited for her reaction.

'A puppy?' She lifted a curious eyebrow. 'That's nice for Poppy. I'm not so sure about Sue. Is she going to be able to cope?'

'With some help. . .' He rubbed his chin and managed to look devastatingly appealing as he lifted dark, coaxing brown eyes. 'I. . .er. . .might need some help. I was wondering if you had a couple of hours free?'

All thought of him vanishing and leaving her to concentrate disappeared. 'Why are you asking me?' She frowned.

'Ken's on call. Sue has her mother staying for the

weekend. And Poppy is. . .well, she's fond of you.'

She gave him a rueful smile. 'I'm flattered—but I suggest you change the day to one convenient with Ken or Sue. I'm afraid I take Aunt Steph shopping on Saturday.'

He looked wounded. 'All day?'

She lied blatantly. 'All day.'

'Mabel's ready to be collected. I could defer it to Sunday. Would Sunday suit?'

'Mabel?' she queried frowningly.

He nodded. 'She's a sort of time-share puppy—sleeping nights at my place and doing days with the Dunwoodys—until the baby's born and settled in.'

Paula sat back and smirked. 'Whose crackpot suggestion was that?'

She was glad to see he looked uncomfortable. 'Mine, as a matter of fact.'

'But you can't time-share animals.'

He laughed softly. 'Watch me.'

'I shall.' She lifted curious eyebrows. 'And how does Sue feel about your idea?'

'Since she's had time to get used to it, pretty good, I think. You see,' he began enthusiastically, 'my theory is Poppy won't feel the inevitable jealousy with a new baby because she'll have the puppy to distract her. As soon as Ken and Sue think they can cope, Mabel can transfer full-time—by which time I'll have her house-trained.'

She resisted the inclination to tell him he looked like the most unsuitable surrogate mother in history! 'Well, I just think it's a crazy idea, that's all. Much better to wait until the baby's older.'

'Which is a bit beside the point, isn't it?'

Paula sighed. 'I hope you're ready for chewed furniture and damp carpets and middle of the night walkies?'

'Oh, don't worry, I'll cope.' He grinned again. 'You'll love her.'

'I'm not being party to this, Sam!'

'She's a Labrador,' he told her, ignoring her resolute protest. 'She'll have a nice, stout, protective bark for guarding the house and practice, and a superb nature for the children. Ideal family dogs.'

Paula felt her toes curling in envy—which she wasn't about to reveal in case he decided she was warming to the hare-brained idea.

'Couldn't manage just an hour, could you?' he murmured, quirking one black eyebrow seductively.

She gazed back at Harry's details, still showing on the computer. 'Give me one good reason why I should help you out. I've my own problems to contend with—and I'm not getting any closer to solving them.'

'As in Harry Bamford?'

'As in Harry.'

'I see the weight reduction's working,' he said dryly.

She sighed. 'I'm trying my best to convince him to slim. But he's got the idea he's unattractive, which seems to act as a kind of defence mechanism against attempting to lose weight.'

'What if I could help resolve the problem for you?' He folded his arms and leaned back in the seat. 'Here's the deal. Help me with Poppy and I'll solve all Harry's weight problems. If I don't succeed you'll have the opportunity to gloat publicly over the fact I've failed.'

'You must be desperate!' she gasped in astonishment.

He shrugged. 'I don't want to disappoint Poppy—this puppy means a lot to her.'

Paula lifted her hands, leaned her elbows defeatedly on her desk and cupped her chin. 'I can hardly refuse the opportunity to see you publicly embarrassed,' she muttered wryly. 'I suppose I could take Aunt Steph shopping on Friday evening. . .'

'Sounds good to me. I'll collect you at eleven.' He unfolded his arms and stood up with a smile from ear to ear. 'Oh, and bring boots—it's a farm.'

Sam didn't collect her—she at least had her say in that. She didn't want Sam anywhere near Aunt Steph, giving her the wrong idea! So she drove to the Dunwoodys' where she had arranged to meet him. Sue had Poppy all set in dungarees and little red wellies, although the late May weather was promising to be wonderful.

'Are you sure you'll be able to cope?' Sue doubtfully produced a travelling bag large enough to hold Poppy's entire wardrobe. '*I've packed disposables* and two changes of clothing. Sam's taken her out before, when Mabel was born, so he knows the ropes. But it seems an awful cheek to haul you away from your weekend. It's really good of you to fill in at the last moment.'

'I'm looking forward to it, Sue. I'll make sure she keeps dry.'

'Take her to the loo as often as you can, Paula. She's not too bad at all if she's reminded.'

Paula opened her arms to Poppy who immediately gave her a huge hug, pressing a battered stuffed dog into her face. She chattered away as Sue translated.

'This is Mabel, she's telling you, the forerunner to Mabel Pup.' She gave a little sigh of wistfulness. 'I do hope this works. Sam's so sure it's going to be a good thing for Poppy. But I have to say, we thought it was a far-fetched suggestion at first. Neither Ken nor I know the first thing about dogs.'

Paula lifted Poppy into her arms. 'Sam worships Poppy, doesn't he?'

Sue smiled. 'Oh, yes, he does, bless him. But then, he just loves kids full stop. That was what was so sad about Jilly.'

Paula looked blank. 'Jilly?'

Sue nodded. 'Dr Jilly Cameron. Sam and Jilly were both intensely committed to keeping the unit in India going, but the sponsorship from a big pharmaceuticals company fell through.' Sue shrugged. 'Look, I hate to talk behind his back, but Sam has always been attracted to women who seem to have sparkling careers ahead of them and don't want to be entrapped by family commitments.'

Just as Sue finished speaking, Sam strode in. He seemed to fill Sue's lounge and Paula just managed to drag her eyes away from the dark shades perched up on a crest of thick black hair the deep green T-shirt covering a broad expanse of chest and tanned, well muscled legs partly covered in denim shorts. A whiff of something extremely heady came her way and she averted her eyes sharply.

Gathering Poppy's things together, she concentrated firmly on clothing. At least she'd chosen to wear something suitable for the day—navy shorts and a white tied-at-the-waist blouse which was cool and yet comfortable for travelling. Not knowing whether Sam had been serious about a farm, she'd thrown jeans and wellies into a bag.

As she bent down with Poppy, she could feel Sam's gaze on her and she was glad Sue chatted away, allowing her stomach to settle from the inevitable lurch it gave when he was in the vicinity.

By the time they were ready, with Poppy firmly strapped into the seat at the back of the Mercedes, it was brilliantly warm.

'Poppy will doze virtually the moment you move off,' Sue called as she waved through the window. 'Have a lovely day.'

'Bye!' shouted Sam as Poppy gurgled happily in the back. Paula turned several times to talk to her, but, as Sue said, the little girl fell asleep instantly.

'She's adorable,' Paula sighed, staring at the golden curls and hamster-like cheeks. As her upward-slanted eyes closed, only the tiny trail of silver dew from her mouth gave any clue that she was a Down's child.

'Adorable and very bright,' Sam emphasized as he drove. 'She knows exactly where we're going. Sue put wellies on her last time she came with us to the farm and yesterday she came and stuffed them in my lap.'

Again, Paula's heart gave a little twist at the softness in his voice, and Sue's remarks on the mysterious Jilly Cameron came back in a disturbing flash. Had he really been hurt by this woman, causing him to react so antagonistically towards her when she had first come? Almost tempted to try to find out, Paula decided to control her curiosity.

'Has Poppy good health as a rule?' she asked instead.

'Fair, I'd say. She's prone to the odd respiratory and ear infection.'

'Sue's amazing to be able to cope.'

He nodded. 'Poppy's started special school and she's doing famously with speech therapy. They've had no trouble in her adapting. She's very loving and even-tempered.'

Paula realized he was especially close to this child. He was a puzzling man. She tried not to study him too hard, yet she remembered the way he had talked at the river bank and the gentleness which had seeped into his voice and the touch of his fingers in her hair.

'How far is the farm?' she asked, peering at the sunlit countryside.

He chuckled. 'Bored already?'

She grinned. 'That's one thing I can't accuse you of—being boring.'

'But you can accuse me of lots of others?'

She nodded. 'Oh, yes, quite easily.'

'Such as?'

'Where would you like me to start?'

He laughed aloud. 'You know what they say, better the devil you know than the one you don't.'

She gazed at him thoughtfully. But what devil did she know? She knew the brusque, single-minded Sam Carlile who reminded her of Jay. But what lay beneath the surface of his antipathy towards her or indeed single professional women? Something, she suspected, that was connected to Jilly Cameron.

Paula tried to concoct a mental picture of the woman, but with very little success. However, she had no difficulty at all in recreating her feelings as she'd stood so close to him with his jacket around her shoulders, when he had held her in his arms and she had lifted her face, her lips opening in automatic response to what she had wanted to do. . .

'You're quiet,' he said suddenly, making her start.

She blushed and realized she'd been deep in thought. 'I was thinking how much I like Warwickshire. How much I feel at home here.'

'Were you? Wouldn't have said you've had much time to acclimatize yet. Four—five weeks, isn't it?'

She smiled wryly. 'Four weeks exactly—tomorrow.'

'Counting the days? Seems like some serious indecision going on there.'

'Regarding the practice?' She turned to smile at him and he met her eyes for a long time, watchful and curious and fleetingly so disturbing that she was the first one to look back at the road. 'No, not with the practice,' she answered haltingly, refraining from saying exactly what or who had been the focus of her recent thoughts.

Determined not to enjoy his company, Paula found herself doing the complete opposite, which she realized with dismay, was not the point of the exercise!

She couldn't possibly look forward to being with Sam

Carlile, could she? It was obvious he liked to bait her. That joke about the devil she knew—she'd caught the look in his eye and it had given her the wretched sensation again,—shivery, tingly. . .

The farm was a dairy farm, and when Holly Johnson met them at the house Sam tugged their change of clothing from the boot, anticipating her suggestion.

'Use my bedroom to change, Paula,' Holly offered. 'Sam can change in the bathroom.'

Paula changed swiftly, smoothing down her jeans and casual shirt. The Johnsons showed them the dairy first and then gave them the grand tour of the Friesian herd. At last they returned to the house and the main attraction; a litter of six golden Labrador puppies romping in the warm kitchen. Holly and Mike Johnson lived in a house filled to the brim with dogs, cats and mice. One mouse in particular scooted across Poppy's boot and her little eyes opened wide in delight.

'Another kid would have screamed blue murder,' Sam whispered proudly to Paula as the puppies smothered them with little nips and licks. 'Isn't she fantastic? No fear at all.'

Paula scooped Poppy into her arms as another barrage of six silky golden-coated pups rolled over them in plump, tail-wagging curiosity.

Mabel, as if she knew, crawled on Poppy's lap and christened her dungarees. Everyone hooted with laughter as Mabel crawled up to Poppy's pink face and licked her repentantly.

'Talk about bonding,' Sam said fervently, kneeling down to help Poppy disentangle herself. 'You two are priceless! Come to Uncle Sam, woofer!'

Paula watched him, seeing the proud gleam in his eye as he held Poppy and the pup, her eyes lingering on the small, inconsequential movements, such as the way he stroked Poppy's hair back from her face and lifted her gently into his arms. Paula had an overwhelmingly pleasurable feeling inside her, heat pervading through her body, a warmth which seemed to have been missing from her life for so long.

Holly and Mike, who had been patients of Sam before they had bought the farm, treated them to chicken pie and home-grown veg. It was a deliriously happy feast, with the Johnsons' own two small children making good company for Poppy. Then came the time to separate Mabel from her family.

'Plenty of newspaper on the floor tonight, Sam,' Holly warned them as they bundled bag and baggage into the Mercedes. 'And she'll be ready for her injections in a week. Until then, keep her in the house and garden away from other dogs. Have you got the tripe I wrapped for you?'

'In the boot,' he muttered. 'Where it belongs.'

'Good luck,' Mike called as Sam revved the engine.

'And you'll need plenty of that,' giggled Paula from the back seat where she sat clutching Mabel's hind quarters on a blanket. Poppy had the best of the deal, bestowed with a soft little black nose and pink tongue.

'Any good at carving up that stuff? Sam asked dismally. 'Reminds me of jellyfish.'

'You're a doctor.' She laughed softly. 'You cut up lots of nastier things in medical school. Besides, I don't think the tripe's the problem. I hope you've an inexhaustible supply of dry socks.'

'You're a great help.'

'I try to be.' She caught the dark and glittering glance in the driving mirror. Could she be mistaken or were the corners of his eyes creased in pleasurable humour?

Poppy chortled as he switched on a CD of Rolf Harris and began to sing the boomerang song. Mabel looked up with one sleepy eye and drifted back off despite the laughter.

Strangely enough, Poppy did not sleep a wink. She was entranced. Her brain was stimulated and her emotions awakened. Paula gazed at the back of the dark head of the man in front of her who had masterminded all this.

And she realized with a shock she had not thought of Jay at all recently. In fact, she could not remember when she had thought of him last.

They dropped a tired Poppy safely into Ken's arms at seven and introduced an equally exhausted Mabel to her new family. Alone with Sam in the surgery car park where she had left the Polo for the day, she asked, 'What about Harry?'

He lifted careless shoulders. 'I'll keep my end of the bargain.' A howling scream made them both jump. 'Good Lord—was that her?' He shot back to his car and frowned in through the window. A heart-rending wail came from inside, and he swept open the door and Mabel leapt into his arms. 'What do you think is wrong?' He studied the tiny mouth and eyes with intense concern.

'Absolutely nothing,' Paula pronounced. 'Other than needing to be cosseted in the absence of Mum.'

He thrust a hand through his hair. 'And I suppose you're about to desert the sinking ship?' He looked at Paula with desperation. 'You wouldn't like to give me a hand settling her in? I don't live far from here. It's left at the crossroads and right at the next roundabout.'

She could feel the warmth of his body against her, and as he laid one large hand on her shoulder she felt the heavy thud of her heart under her ribs. No, said a small voice inside, whatever you do, don't agree—make up some excuse that you've got to get home. Then almost immediately came another voice, the illogical, tremulous voice trapped deeply inside her which had long since been quieted. Since Emily and Jay, she had lost track of it, lost the warmth and excitement that it had brought to her life. Did it show in her eyes? All the hidden emotion was there, just behind their surface—emotion dampened by grief and separation and secured even more in the chamber of the past by a resolution that she would never allow herself to be hurt again.

'I know it's a bit much to ask,' he murmured, his eyes searching her face. 'And it's been a long day.' He fell silent. 'Forget it,' he mumbled. 'I know what you're thinking. And it's true. I've taken on the responsibility of the dog—no one else seemed to think it was such a good idea. I'll have to sort this one out.'

Paula could not resist smiling. 'I suppose I could cut up that stuff in the boot for you. But only if you've household gloves and a sharp knife. And I don't propose to sit all evening nursemaiding a puppy—'

'Excellent,' he interrupted her with a sigh of relief. 'Just half an hour, that's all. Promise.'

A promise that began to fade as the Mercedes turned into a dirt track and Sam parked, leapt out of his car, unlatched a gate and tipped Mabel on to the square of neat green grass in front of a cottage. 'Phew, just in time,' he sighed as Paula drew the Polo by the fence and joined them. 'Oh, by the way,' he murmured huskily, 'welcome to Candle Cottage. Bit of a mess, I'm afraid. I haven't had a chance to do much to it over the last eighteen months. I'm thinking about selling, actually.'

'Because you're returning to Delhi?'

He glanced away from Mabel and found her eyes. 'Did Sue tell you?'

'No, my aunt,' she admitted, wondering if he was going to fill in the missing details, but he merely looked down at Mabel before sweeping her up into his arms and thrusting his key in the door. 'Kitchen's on the right down the hall,' he said. 'Help yourself.'

She was curious to see what this man surrounded himself with. Cosy, small, creaky and squeaky, the kitchen possessed an Aga—no surprises—and the window looked out onto apple trees. Nothing spoke much of ownership. . .it was, as he'd said, a house waiting for attention. Sam followed her in as Mabel padded around the kitchen, sniffing her new home.

'Pool little mite.' Paula bent to draw her finger along the pudgy spine and wobbly limbs. 'Where's your mum?'

'She'll have to make do with me. She can sleep on the bed tonight.'

Paula looked up at him ruefully. 'Someone won't be getting much sleep.' She stood, smiling softly up at him as he gazed down at her, the dark eyes so full of vibrant intensity that her heart shifted treacherously inside her.

Quite suddenly he reached out, drawing her up against him in one slow, powerful movement. It was so unexpected that she had no time to resist as he drew her into his arms. 'I've been waiting to do this all day,' he said, almost regretfully, as she gave in without protest to the warm sensations running through her, wondering if she was in the middle of a dream.

'I haven't been able to take my eyes off you,' he said, and lifted a hand to run his fingers through the fine blonde silk of her hair, trailing them softly down her neck. She sighed responsively, which was her undoing as he bent down, teasing her lips with his. She opened them and gave way to the spiral of pleasure which was turning into heat beyond her control.

'Sam. . .' she whispered imploringly as his lips searched hers, brushing softly. 'I don't think I'm ready for this. . .'

'Nor am I,' he agreed in a tight whisper. 'But I'm doing it anyway.' He tipped up her chin, his touch making her tremble, and he bent to kiss her deeply, in hot, open mouthed need as she dragged her arms around his neck and kissed him back, her body shuddering against him as her fingers roved his hair and fluttered over his scalp.

He lifted his head slowly, sweeping her throat with soft kisses, her chin and her mouth, and, gently easing her away, he sighed. She realized with a shock she wanted to be kissed, wanted it more than anything else in the world at this moment, but she pushed away, her hands shaking against the firm, warm muscle of his chest.

'Paula, stay. . .'

'Sam, what are we doing?' she gasped softly, her grey eyes confused. 'One minute we're flying at each other—'

'The next you're kissing me. . .'

'I'm—kissing—you!' she spluttered, and she found herself trapped as she tried to push away, the strong arms linked around her and the pound of his heart beating against her own.

'I had no intention of this happening,' he said, and she stopped struggling and gazed into his eyes as a look of bewilderment and yearning came into them and made her powerless to move. She was having difficulty in thinking of anything except the way he had made her feel, the pleasure of his touch on her skin, the kiss which had melted her into someone she hardly recognized, someone warm and alive, the someone she had lost and thought she would never find again after Emily.

He was silent for a moment, before drawing a wisp of blonde hair from her eyes with the same gentle action he had used with Poppy. Then he drew her even closer and she looked up at him, exchanging surprised, apprehensive smiles, and then his head came down and she closed her eyes. The next kiss was slow and adventurous, his tongue probing her mouth open with sweet insist-

ence, as she let herself drown in the sensation of total
unreality.

No, this was the last thing she had wanted, said the
sensible comfortable, guarded self, the protective half
which had seen her safely through the years of despair
after Jay and Emily. But it was a weak voice, weakened
by the power of the lips caressing hers, the hands travelling over her spine, bringing her body against him with
shocking and startling pleasure.

As if she were waking from a spell, her eyes flipped
open to see his staring down at her, his lips a fraction
away from her own, the expression in his face seeming
to be a reflection of her own fragmented sensations.

'I didn't intend this to happen,' he whispered. 'I didn't
want this to happen.'

'Then why—?' she began, only to stop as he kissed
her again and her fingers began to thread wildly through
his dark, thick hair, exploring the solid, warm shape of
his skull, the long, tough muscle of his bent neck and
the tiny throb of pulse that appeared under her fingers
as she brought her hands to cup his jaw, connecting
them somehow, against their wishes, with a frightening
force beyond either of them.

'Oh, Paula. . .' he whispered, a groan coming deeply
from his throat as the next invasion of his lips over hers
brought a cry from her, as his hands threaded through
her hair almost roughly.

Her mind felt as if it had turned to cotton wool. Mabel
whimpered and scrabbled over their ankles, for one
second bringing them back to the real world, but not
before his fingers had begun to wander over her body,
thrilling her with yearning and desire that made her
helpless in his grasp.

'You're so lovely to look at at,' he muttered against
her cheek, his skin hot and urgent against her own. 'So
feminine. . .'

Paula was suddenly brought back to earth by the words, for Sam had made his real feelings for her quite plain. 'Hard-hearted career woman' was now being translated as lovely to look at, feminine, because she was a woman at his disposal, a woman reacting to the attraction of a body which seemed to have splintered every sensible thought in her head by the sensual energy that flowed from it.

As he kissed the hollow of her throat and brought his lips to her ear, licking the sensitively smooth skin which made her shudder and shiver at the same time, she found the will from somewhere to push him gently away. His dark-shadowed, misty eyes came up to meet hers.

'Sam, I think I'd better go.'

'Why?'

'You know why. This isn't making any sense.'

He leaned his forehead slowly against hers. 'Does it have to?'

'For me,' she whispered, 'yes, it does. We know nothing about one another. We don't even like one another—'

'I've never said that.'

'You don't have to.'

'Then what are we doing here—like this. . .?'

She pushed away again, forcing herself to ignore the hard muscle beneath her fingertips, the throb which was still pulsating through her body and the terrible ache that seemed to have resurrected itself deep down inside. She shifted against him and finally he let her go. Without a word she made her way out of the cottage and into the evening, blinking as she clutched inwardly at any straw which would obliterate the memory of his hooded expression and the hot, sensual tug of desire which even now called her back against her will.

CHAPTER FOUR

IT WAS like living with a grumbling volcano, and when it went quiet the threat seemed almost worse than the rumbling of lava. Not that this particular volcano had suggested the promised miracle cure for Harry Bamford, but then, thought Paula, had she really expected any?

Sam had needed help with Poppy and she had been conveniently on hand. What had happened at the cottage afterwards was something they both regretted—obviously. Nearly two weeks of dodging one another had proven it!

As Valerie Curry stood in Reception now, her eyes red with tears, she produced a neat, handwritten list of her recent ills and waited for Paula to study them. Sam, who had been initially waylaid by a patient, looked at Paula.

'Have you a patient?' he asked with a frown, taking Valerie's elbow and steering her to one side. 'I've a house call to make—could you see Mrs Curry for me?'

'Oh, I know I haven't made an official appointment, but I need to make sure,' sobbed the woman, looking pleadingly at them both. 'I need to know if there's something wrong with me. I want the truth.'

Sam caught Paula's eye, then he glanced at his watch. 'Mrs Curry, I've five minutes to spare, but then I must be on my way.'

Paula gestured to her empty room. She had already spotted that fatigue and headache came at the top of the list, insomnia and sweating in the middle and ulcer, cancer of the stomach and coeliac disease at the bottom. There was no mention of hypochondria, however, a mal-

56

aise which was becoming more evident than ever as time went on, though seemingly unnoticed by Valerie.

Paula tapped her keyboard and brought up the thirty-nine-year-old housewife's notes. On the screen she saw that each of the doctors had been consulted throughout Mrs Curry's varied medical history.

Sam said tentatively, 'And your concerns this morning are. . .?'

'Any one of the last three are my own personal diagnosis,' responded Valerie, hugging her handbag. She was a pale, slender woman, with short reddish hair, and was rather overdressed in a thick cardigan on a beautiful June morning.

'What makes you think you have cancer or coeliac disease?' Paula asked curiously.

'Well,' said Valerie worriedly, 'I'm sweating terribly. I seem to have an allergy to cereals because I come out in a kind of prickly heat rash when I eat them. And I've lost weight. About half a stone lately. My friend's little girl is a coeliac, you see, and I've all the same symptoms.'

'But you also suggest cancer of the stomach,' interrupted Sam patiently.

'Loss of appetite, pain here. . .' She pressed her hand over the cardigan near her heart. 'And what I'm most worried about. . .bleeding.' She almost whispered the word in Paula's direction. 'You know, when you spend a penny? I'm in a terrible state, I'm afraid, but I've had lots of things wrong with me in the last few years and it just seems to be getting worse.'

Paula digested the information on her computer monitor and realized that perhaps she had better try to deal with her patient's main concern which seemed to be causing her worry. 'I'd like to examine you, Mrs Curry.'

'Well, then,' said Sam, smiling what looked like a relieved smile, 'I'll leave you to Dr Harvie,

Mrs Curry, if there's nothing more I can do. . .?'

Paula flicked him a wry smile. 'Thank you, Dr Carlile.'

'Ooh, yes—thank you,' effused Valerie Curry. 'I'm sorry to have detained you.'

As Sam slid out of the door with a faint smile over his shoulder, Paula forced her mind away from the sight of the broad shoulders and thick dark hair which seemed to have occupied the major moments of her contemplative thinking these days and attuned herself to her patient.

'Perhaps you'd like to explain in your own words what's been happening since you had your hysterectomy,' she suggested with a sigh. 'Two years ago, wasn't it?'

The woman sniffed, dried her eyes and began to undress, readily going into detail about her fibroids, her heavy periods, iron deficiency anaemia and her subsequent operation to remove her womb.

Paula examined her; Mrs Curry appeared to have no pain as she palpitated her abdomen, telling Paula in great detail and using the correct clinical terms for the procedures connected with her hysterectomy.

There was, however, Paula discovered, a problem her patient had not described. 'How long have you had these haemorrhoids?' Paula asked as the stream of vivid description abated for a few seconds.

'Haemorrhoids—piles, you mean?' Her patient seemed surprised. 'You mean, the itching and the pain down there—?'

'Have you experienced any constipation?

'After my op, yes. I never really got back to normal.'

'And now, since you're not eating cereal or wholemeal bread, obviously a large proportion of your diet is lacking roughage. Hence the constipation and this slight bleeding, causing haemorrhoids and loss of weight.'

Her patient seemed lost for words for once.

'Mrs Curry, I think we should try to clear up this problem first, which we can do quite easily. I'd like you to return to eating cereal and wholemeal bread again, and double up on the fresh fruit and vegetables. This will cure the constipation, and I'll prescribe a soothing ointment for the haemorrhoids meanwhile.'

'You don't think the bleeding is cancer, then?'

'I think you have what is known as an anal varicose vein which has become swollen because of the repeated pressure within it, through straining. Your bleeding, I'm quite sure, comes from this. To cure it, you must begin again to eat a more sensible diet.'

'But what about my allergy? What if I'm a coeliac?'

Paula tapped out a prescription. 'Did you know that coeliac disease is almost always diagnosed in infancy or early childhood?'

Valerie Curry shrugged. 'No, not really.'

'In very rare cases, when a mild form is not detected in infancy, a person's growth could be stunted as a result of the small intestine coming into allergic contact with gluten. You had no such problems as a child or teenager?'

Her patient shook her head. 'But I do have a rash. . .'

'Which could be caused by any number of things, from stress and worry over a condition you most certainly haven't acquired, to washing your clothes in a powder which is not suitable for your skin. Try getting back to eating sensibly, creating healthier habits and put out of your mind any worries over cancer.'

A fleeting expression of surprise came over the older woman's face. 'My husband has done the shopping and washing recently as I haven't been feeling very well. I wonder if he's using cheap washing powder?'

Almost before Paula could tear off the prescription from the printer, Valerie Curry, with a look of determination on her face, had reached the door.

'Mrs Curry, don't forget your prescription!'

'That's what you get for letting a man in the kitchen.' She sighed, coming back and taking it. 'I've been feeling itchy all over lately. I have such sensitive skin.'

Paula felt sorry for Mr Curry and for having passed the buck because it probably wasn't his fault at all either. But, in view of the half-hour which had just disappeared from her timetable, she felt marginally justified as she waded through her appointments during the rest of the day.

Tricia, one of the receptionists, came in to see her before she locked the front door. 'No late emergencies, Dr Harvie. OK to lock up?'

'Fine, thanks, Tricia. Has everyone gone?'

'The doctors Dunwoody are out in the garden with Mabel and Poppy. Other than last minute emergencies, we're all finished.'

'I'll probably go and say goodnight, so leave the side door open, will you?'

'Will do. Night, Dr Harvie.'

Paula sat back with a sigh. The garden beckoned her, as did a last cuddle with Poppy and Mabel, and she went to sketch on a coat of peachy lipstick and brush her hair before going out.

She had worn a slender ivory cotton shift today to keep cool at work and now she was grateful of its comfort as she walked in the garden, the air tingling her bare arms pleasantly. Poppy and Mabel came crashing into her legs amidst gales of giggles. It had been almost two weeks since Mabel had made her home with the Dunwoodys—two weeks since Paula's intimate brush with Sam Carlile and her subsequent escape. . .

Sue came hurrying down the garden, treading rather

heavily, looking tired, Paula thought. 'Time for a coffee?' she asked, smiling cheerfully. 'Ken's just gone on a call, and I need a break before preparing dinner.'

Back in the house, Sue put on the kettle. 'I'm feeling quite shattered,' she confessed. 'My ankles are up a bit, too.'

Paula had noticed this. She occupied Poppy at the kitchen table with crayons and a book whilst Mabel flopped into her basket by the Aga. 'You're probably doing a bit too much, but then you don't need me to tell you this.'

'I think I'll cut down to two days in surgery, if that's all right with you?'

'That's what I'm here for. And so far none of your patients have objected—not even Valerie Curry this morning.'

Sue rolled her eyes as she poured coffee. 'Oh, no, what was wrong this time?'

'Don't ask,' laughed Paula, watching Sue plodding around the kitchen to mop up a puddle on the floor. 'Shouldn't Mabel have gone home with Sam?' she asked thoughtfully.

'Oh, he'll be here any moment. He's had a phone call from a colleague in India. I think they're trying to persuade him to return. Sam said he'd wait until after the baby. But. . .well. . .no one has actually said, "If this is a Down's baby, too". Of course it would mean all the difference. . .' Suddenly Sue buried her face in her hands.

'Oh, Sue!' Paula stood up and slid an arm around her shoulders. 'I'm sorry. I didn't realize you were worrying. You seem so in control.'

Sue wiped her eyes and gave a muffled laugh. 'I'm being totally unreasonable, I know. I took the decision to have another and not to have the triple blood test or an amnio. I could have stopped with Poppy. She's such a dear. But I do...do so want a child who's... Oh, Paula—I'm sorry to lay all this on you. But I can't worry Ken. He's been such a love, and yet he didn't want to take the risk of another child.'

'I'm sure everything is going to turn out just fine,' Paula said reassuringly. 'Your instinct was to have a baby. I'm sure it was a right one. I think you're worrying unnecessarily and that won't do either you or the baby any good. My advice—professionally—is to enjoy this pregnancy. Have you tried playing Handel's Water Music next to your tummy?'

They both laughed, and Sue gave a deep sigh. 'Thank you for listening, Paula.' Just then, a loud rap came at the door. 'Oh, that's Sam for Mabel, I expect.'

Paula laid a hand on Sue's shoulder. 'Stay where you are; I'll get it.'

As Paula went through the house, her heart picked up speed. Absurd though it was, she stopped for a few seconds by the hall mirror and drew her fingers through her hair. She couldn't help it, but she was feeling flushed and excited—until she opened the door.

'Just what,' Sam demanded in a voice which crackled with anger, 'gives you the temerity to tell one of my patients I've been feeding them dope? And who the blazes do you think you are in coming to this practice and laying down the law?'

Shaken, Paula stood her ground. 'I haven't the least idea what you're talking about.'

'Haven't you?' He narrowed his eyes fiercely. 'One of my patients has just accused me of prescribing an addictive drug to her child because that nice Dr Harvie had warned her off it and suggested some absurd herbal weed.'

'Do you realize you're shouting?'

He glared at her. 'It's the only way with women like you.'

'What did you say?'

'You heard,' he erupted. 'Ambitious, selfish, career-oriented female doctors who seem to think they have a God-given right to minister to the whole world.'

'I suggest you go away and calm down,' Paula interrupted icily. 'Because before I discuss anything with you I shall expect an apology for your last comment. And I mean—an apology.'

She then closed the door firmly in Sam's face.

'What was all that about?' Sue appeared, frowning. 'What in heaven's name was Sam shouting for?'

Paula sighed, folding her shaky arms protectively around herself. 'I don't know. Something about a patient of his and my telling this patient her child was taking an addictive drug and prescribing a quack remedy instead. I honestly can't think what he's talking about.' She shuddered. 'He didn't give me a chance to respond, just bombarded me with insults.'

Sue frowned. 'Oh, Paula, I'm amazed. He's not usually so insensitive.'

Paula shrugged. Then when she saw Sue's dismay she managed a smile. 'Please don't worry. . .it's probably nothing. I'm sorry you had to overhear.'

Sue shook her head earnestly. 'I'll go and have a word with him.'

Paula reached out and gripped her arm, horrified at the thought. 'No, absolutely not, Sue. I can fight my own battles, thanks. I should hate him to think I was a whinger. Now, come on back to Poppy and I'll leave you in peace. My instructions are to put your feet up until Ken arrives home.'

Paula guided Sue back to Poppy and Mabel, then shepherded them all into the front room and left them listening to a musical on TV. When she walked back into the surgery the place was deserted. She locked up and reversed the Polo from the car park.

Halfway back to Warwick, she stopped the car, reversed into a field and drove back the way she had come. She couldn't rest, and perhaps now Sam would have cooled down enough to be approached without a full-scale shouting match.

His car was not parked outside Candle Cottage. Nor was there any sign of life from inside when she peered in through the windows. And then she had a thought. He would have, of course, returned to collect Mabel—wouldn't he? Perhaps he had been in the surgery—even watched her leave,—then gone back to Sue's. After all, he wouldn't let Sue down.

A deduction which proved to be correct as she drove back into the car park and discovered the Mercedes parked there. She used her side door key, realizing very soon someone else was in the surgery because the alarm had been switched off. Then she heard a little yelp and a scuffle, and Mabel waddled towards her over the waiting room carpet.

'Hello, sweetheart.' Paula lifted her into her arms and kissed her silky head. 'Where's that angry bear of a master of yours?' she murmured, and trod warily along the hall.

He was sitting in his consulting room. The table light was switched on, reflecting his features in dark shadow and unflattering light. His dark eyes gleamed. His black hair framed his face like a cameo, and his shoulders revealed every inch of wrathful body language as she walked in.

'Can you bring yourself to discuss the matter in a reasonable manner?' she asked tightly.

'Reasonable?' he growled. 'You don't know the meaning of the word.'

'Insulting people doesn't help.'

'Oh, if a few comments—'

' "Selfish, career-oriented female doctors". . . If I said

that about you, that I thought you were a self-opinionated, stubborn, judgemental man, would you like it?'

He shrugged. 'Some of it would fit, I suppose.'

'Some of it?' She snorted. 'You didn't give me a chance to defend myself. All you could do was bandy insults around.'

'I'm sorry if I've offended your sense of self-worth,' he retorted swiftly. 'But I've run into inflated female ego before—and come off pretty badly.'

She stared at him incredulously. 'And because of a past experience—which has nothing at all to do with me—you're willing to tar me with the same brush?'

'After today, I think I've probably every right to assume the worst,' he threw back at her. 'Call me prejudice, if you like, but every female I seem to have run into in medicine has been the same. You're not here five minutes and you're already interfering with my patients—'

'Stop right there!' She held up a hand, though it was shaking. Determinedly taking a deep breath, she sat in the patient's chair, lowering Mabel to the floor at her feet. 'Do you mind telling me just who you are talking about?'

'Alison Lawrence, of course,' he threw at her.

Paula stared at him uncomprehendingly. 'You'd better explain. I'm none the wiser.'

He leaned back in his chair, pinning his fingers together under his chin. She sensed suppressed anger coming over to her in waves. 'I was expecting a call from Delhi,' he said curtly. 'I've been waiting for weeks to hear from a colleague and it is very important we speak. However. . .' he looked up darkly, and his eyes glittered angrily. . .'the doorbell went. I opened it. It was Alison Lawrence. She had an empty bottle of Phenergan in her hand and she thrust it in my face. She said, if it hadn't been for you, Jamie would be hooked on it. That she'd phoned some wretched crank or other you'd put her into contact with and she'd started Jamie on some flower or something, for heaven's sake!'

He almost snarled the next part. 'Meanwhile my phone was ringing. When I finally got to it, the line was dead. I rang the number to find out who had been calling and it had been from Delhi. The one phone call I couldn't afford to miss—all because of your damn interference with my patients.'

'Let's stick to Alison Lawrence, shall we?' She rose slowly and leaned forward, resting her palms on his desk, gazing levelly into the intransigent eyes. 'I had no idea it was you who prescribed Phenergan for Jamie, only that he seemed to be having too much of it. Mrs Lawrence was using it as a permanent sedative which was making Jamie irritable and not helping his under-lying condition of hyperactivity.'

'It was for me to make that decision—not you,' he protested angrily. 'You should have asked me to review the treatment with you.'

'That's not exactly easy, lately. I hardly see you. And you were only too eager to relegate Valerie Curry to me. Is it only at your discretion that I should see certain patients and not others? If it is, you'd better start drawing up a list!'

'That's absurd,' he said sharply. 'It's just like a woman to allow a simple matter to get out of hand—'

'It obviously *isn't* simple. Your prejudice is compli-cated enough to make our relationship quite untenable. What am I to do if one of your patients—other than Valerie Curry—insists on being treated by me?'

'Discover the whole of the story before you start handing out advice,' he barked back at her. 'For instance, did Alison Lawrence tell you I had twice called at her home and left a note she should ring me? Did she tell you that she had persuaded a locum we had here to prescribe her the Phenergan—despite my calls and repeated requests to come in and see me?'

Paula swallowed sharply, slowly sitting down. 'No, she didn't.'

'The woman's evaded me. Deliberately. Didn't it occur to you for one moment that I might have tried to get hold of her?'

Paula hesitated, realizing she had been totally won over by Alison Lawrence's story. She said in a defensive voice, 'I suppose I went from instinct. I've researched enough on the subject to know I wouldn't want my child taking large and unnecessary doses of promethazine.'

He lifted a contemptuous eyebrow. 'Clearly it's a choice you don't have to make.'

Paula felt the pain encapsulate her in a familiar and almost unbearable surge of suppressed grief. 'I might have had to,' she said shakily, her eyes suddenly filling with an unbearable salty heat, 'if my daughter had lived. She weighed a little over four pounds when she was born two months prematurely. If she had lived. . .if I had been given the chance of raising her. . .' She swallowed, forcing back the tears, tears she long ago thought had dried but were still achingly real in her soul, aching to hold that dear little bundle in her arms as she had for a fleeting half hour during the short, discreet funeral service in the hospital chapel.

She cleared her throat. 'During the months I carried her, I thought every day of how I should care for her, protect her, love her. Hence, as a mother—for however brief a time—I feel qualified emotionally and professionally to advise Mrs Lawrence on Jamie. I'm sorry I didn't think to ask you about the case. It seemed, at first, quite straightforward. I see now there was more to it. . .'

She just managed to keep herself together. But inside

she was tearing apart, aching, grieving all over again. Sam's remark had caused the old pain to return and grip her in its violent fist, ever more violent as the years had distanced her from Emily's death and she had schooled herself to live again.

At the door, she cast him one last look. 'The herb Mrs Lawrence was talking about is probably evening primrose oil—a source of gamma-linolenic acid. I know it's not high on every doctor's list of treatments, but I happen to think it's a reasonable alternative—' her voice finally broke, and she walked out. Almost ran. Possibly she would have if it had not been for her pride.

Why had she blurted out about Emily? Just to prove a point? And yet in proving the point she had only humiliated herself.

She fell into the Polo and steamed out of the car park. All the memories came pouring into her mind. She had told herself she hated Jay—but in the end she'd only felt an emptiness, a disbelief that a man could keep two relationships going so harmoniously at the same time and not have a single twinge of conscience throughout it all. True, Emily's death had affected him, but a man could have no conception of what it felt like to give birth and lose a child within the space of a few hours.

Now at least she understood the resemblance between Sam and Jay. Their unshakeable belief in themselves to be right. Well, the Phenergan affair had made her look like all the other women he so obviously despised.

If only she had given a little more thought to the reality of the case and a little less credence to Alison Lawrence! Today's lesson was one she wouldn't forget in a hurry.

At home that evening, she ran herself a deep bath, putting the bleeper on the shelf, knowing that she was on call. No doubt as soon as she put a toe in the bath water someone would need attention.

She lay in the soothing water and let the tears fall, trying to overcome the debilitating, dreadful ache created when Sam had brought Emily's ghost to life.

For once, she did not mind being persuaded from the tub when the phone rang. She had soaked for long enough and cried for long enough. In a towel and flip flops, she answered it, putting on a brave face for Aunt Steph, who was calling to say she was staying over with a friend for the night.

Afterwards, feeling she should make some repair to her puffy eyes, she sat with an assortment of creams, smoothing them into her skin, and changed into white slacks and an Indian cotton print top.

The phone went again and this time it was Bella, working late at the surgery. She apologised. 'Two possible calls. Might be an idea if you came in for the notes, Dr Harvie. One lady has SLE and quite a complicated medical history.'

In fifteen minutes Paula arrived at Struan House and settled down to examine Tracey Horley's notes. Sam's bold, powerful handwriting met her gaze. 'Vasculitis— rash, fever, malaise, weight loss'—this last remark underlined—caused Paula to sit down whilst she read that twenty-eight-year-old Tracey had been diagnosed two years previously from haematological investigations. Sam had taken over her treatment when she had first signed on with the surgery a year previously.

Tracey's treatment consisted of drug therapy. Systemic lupus erythematosus had not yet involved the young woman's kidneys, and Sam had underlined again the strict regime he had managed her on; corticosteroids, analgesics and anti-inflammatory drugs.

The irony of the situation was, she would have to

phone Sam. It was the last thing in the world she wanted
to do after this morning.

Half hoping he would not be at Candle Cottage, she
rang him. His deep, resonant voice came back firmly.
'I'll meet you there,' he said, and put down the phone.
That was all. No time to say she would go on to the
second call—and if she didn't turn up. . .

Paula sighed. It was going to be a long evening.

When she arrived at the terraced house just outside of
Struan, Sam pulled up almost simultaneously. With a
last glance in her driving mirror at her dewy eyes, she
pushed up her chin and went to meet him.

'I thought it better we see Tracey together,' he said
in a surprisingly pleasant manner. 'You may well have
her again in the summer.'

Surprised but not fooled, Paula nodded as Tracey,
wrapped in a beach robe, came to the door.

'We've just come back from holiday—early,' Tracey
said urgently before either of them could speak.
'Come in.'

She pushed back her long hair as they sat in the
lounge. It was then Paula noticed her face, swollen and
disfigured by a rash.

'I know what you're going to say,' Tracey murmured
miserably. 'It's my own fault, isn't it? I sunbathed.'

'Where did you go?' Sam asked, beginning to examine the damage over her blistered shoulders.

'Greece—and it was good weather,' admitted Tracey.
'When we went I was determined I wouldn't sunbathe,
and then my boyfriend Mike said half an hour wouldn't
hurt. But it was terrible. To be honest, I stuck the heat
out for a couple more days and then I couldn't wait to
get home. I know you'll be furious with me for dis-
obeying you—after all you've done for me, Dr Carlile.'

'It's too late now to be furious,' Sam reprimanded

gently as Paula came to examine the blemished skin and sensitive sunburn. 'There's not a lot I can do.' After examining her thoroughly, he began to write a prescription for corticosteroid cream and a repeat prescription for the drugs she was already taking. Use this sparingly, avoid any further exposure to sunlight.' He emphasized firmly, '*Any* sunlight!'

Paula was relieved to see no sign of pleurisy, but the girl was extremely slender and she began to complain of joint inflammation in her elbows. 'It's such a weird disease,' She sighed as she sat back, looking very tired. 'Why can't I have something ordinary?'

'No disease is ordinary,' remarked Sam philosophically. 'Every illness is inconvenient to the people who have it. Perhaps we can organize some physio to prevent your skin from becoming uncomfortably tight.'

Tracey nodded. 'If you think it will help. I just wish I could sunbathe, that's all, like other women. They all had fabulous tans in Greece.'

Paula smiled. 'When you're over this bout you'll look pale and interesting with that lovely sprinkling of freckles.' It was cold consolation for the poor girl, Paula thought as Sam and she took their leave. Joints, muscles, skin, blood vessels—SLE had no preference, and it always took its victim by surprise,—ironically often young women whose priority was a healthy tan. Since sunlight was the foremost aggravating factor, symptoms were often ignored before an experience such as this drove home the severity.

'Vanity, vanity,' Sam muttered at the car, pushing in his case. 'All is vanity.'

'She is young,' Paula protested. 'And most women do want a tan. She's really a very sweet girl.'

He closed his car door and leanted against it. 'She is—but vexing. This isn't the first time. We've had one or two alarms, which is one reason I thought I'd better

join you tonight, to make sure you were aware of the
case should you be called in again, and—' he looked
at her levelly '—there's another reason I wanted to see
you. I realize it must have taken courage to talk about
Emily today. I just wish I hadn't made it so difficult for
you. Alison Lawrence got the better of us both for a bit.
She unfortunately caused a misunderstanding neither of
us was prepared to spot at first glance. All I can say is
that I'm sorry, Paula. The last thing I wanted to do was
force you to talk about your daughter.'

Somehow her heart melted, and she nodded, biting
down on her lip. 'I don't very often—I don't really
know why I did today.'

'Perhaps because you needed to?' He said gently.
'Her death must have been a terrible shock for you.'

She nodded. 'The possibility of losing Emily was
something that never entered my head. I couldn't believe
it had happened to me. It was over so quickly. There
was no reason why I couldn't have completed my pregnancy—I felt so cheated.' The soft sunshine mellowed
around them as she leaned beside him, feeling the warm
support of the car beneath her spine. She looked up at
him, and he was watching her, waiting. 'I wish I could
say Jay and I grew closer after her death, but he was
already involved with someone else. I think we should
have grieved together. . .instead the rift between us
deepened.'

'Was there no chance of a reconciliation?' he asked
quietly.

She looked up at him. 'I trusted Jay. I thought I knew
him. I tried to understand why he had deceived me so
early on in our marriage. He was a good doctor and he
worked hard. We met whilst I was training. . .he was a
consultant and I was impressionable—perhaps even
naive. Even so, I thought we had something special.'
She stopped, shrugging, folding her arms around herself.

CAROL WOOD 73

'It was a long time ago...but every so often...' She shook her head, her throat tightening as she tried to compose herself.

'The grief goes on, doesn't it? There's no miracle cure. Only time.'

She nodded. 'The bad days arrive less often. Days when I wonder if I had contributed to Emily's death or I think that if I'd been able to handle the discovery of Jay's adultery more maturely Emily might have survived—'

'And you know she wouldn't. But still you feel guilty. And, until you learn to talk about Emily, you will.'

'Yes.' He seemed to understand, and he reached across and touched her arm. Just a gentle, small stroke.

The silence deepened around them until she realized he was staring at her with eyes which were softened by sympathy and compassion. She gave him a tentative smile. 'Well, I suppose I had better make my last call.'

'Feel like some company?' he said in a manner which posed no challenge and touched her for its sincerity and thoughtfulness.

'Yes, I'd like that,' she murmured, and he gave her a smile which made her realize she had trusted him enough to open her heart. Just a little. But it was enough.

'I've tried several remedies from the chemist for cystitis,' Marjorie Dent, a widow of sixty-eight, admitted as she chatted to Paula and Sam in her tiny kitchenette. The sheltered housing was adequate for one, but very small, Paula observed.

'Are you drinking plenty of fluid?' Paula noticed a cold cup of tea on the table and several sachets of home cure remedies.

'Oh, yes,' Mrs Dent responded. 'Dr Dunwoody told me the more I drink the better. Trouble is, then I'm always spending pennies. I just potter on in my own way when this happens and try to buy something without bothering the doctor.'

Marjorie's chronic inflammation of the bladder had not responded to the over-the-counter preparations and Paula saw that trimethoprim had been used before by Ken Dunwoody in treatment of his patient. As Majorie was in such discomfort Paula began her on the antibiotic again.

'Have you someone who can go to the chemist for you?' she asked.

'My next door neighbour. He'll be able to go to the chemist. It's open late tonight.'

'Good. And I'd like you to have follow-up urine studies,' Paula urged. 'I'll have a word with the district nurse to pop in and talk about managing the problem with you.'

'Oh, don't trouble, Dr Harvie,' Mrs Dent prevaricated, looking up at Sam. 'I don't like to be a nuisance.'

'The DN's are more than happy to be of some support,' he said with a smile that obviously had the same effect on Marjorie as it had on Paula. 'And they'll sort out any problems for you, so you won't have to wait for one of us to turn up in an emergency.'

'Oh, that would be lovely,' sighed Majorie, blushing. 'Would you two young people like a cup of tea?'

'We'll leave you to organize your prescription,' said Sam. 'Another time, perhaps.'

At the cars, Sam leaned an arm on the Polo roof. 'Well, I'd better let you get back home,' he said, looking at her thoughtfully. And, then, the most surprising thing of the day happened. 'I don't want to intrude,' he murmured. 'But next time you feel like talking about Emily, I'm here. Will you remember that?'

She nodded, aware he was searching her face with warm and gentle eyes. Aware, too, that almost imperceptibly their relationship had changed. But she was just too tired to try to figure out in what way.

Paula found herself twice as busy the following hectic week.

She was pleased. The activity kept her distanced and focused. Hence, the frenetic life of Struan House was something she could plough into with energy. And she was beginning to know Struan well—well enough to feel at home with the country folk and their families.

Sally Walker phoned her early in the week, feeling unwell. She was complaining of breathlessness and severe indigestion. Paula didn't like the sound of it. 'Have you spoken to Dr Carlie?' she asked, still over-cautious about Sam's patients.

'The receptionist told me it's Dr Carlile's day off today,' Sally informed her, gulping air. 'They're trying to get him on his mobile.'

Paula said she would visit immediately. She made the journey to Warwick and Sally's beautiful Tudor house, and found Sam's car was parked in the drive next to Sally's blue Vauxhall. Bella must have managed to contact him, and Paula felt relieved as she walked in to discover him examining Sally on the sofa.

'I've checked the baby and BP,' he said without preamble as Selwyn joined them. 'I know you're not going to like this, Sally, but I'm going to admit you, just to be on the safe side.'

Surprisingly Sally nodded, holding her shoulder with her hand. 'I don't really care any more, Dr Carlile,' she choked. 'I seem to have pain all over. Even in my neck and face. It's really odd.' She tugged up her face to Paula. 'I'm sorry to have dragged you both out. It's probably just a bad bout of indigestion.'

Paula squeezed her hand and, looking at Sam, she knew exactly what was in his mind. In theory, Sally was complaining of indigestion, but the pain she went on to describe was heavy or 'locking'. Her neck, jaw and shoulder were uncomfortable and she complained of dizziness and shortness of breath. Sam, she was sure, had already arrived at the same conclusion. Their patient's heart was suspect and hospital tests alone would rule out the worrying concern of Sally's symptoms.

Sam made an emergency call to Warwick General and the ambulance arrived soon, by which time Selwyn had packed a bag and locked the house. Paula was grateful he did not ask them too many questions but was level-headed enough to keep Sally cheerful.

Sam shot ahead to the hospital as Selwyn went in the ambulance with Sally. By the time Paula arrived, Sally had been admitted into Accident and Emergency and within minutes they had transferred her to a cardiac unit.

'I can't imagine what's gone wrong,' Selwyn moaned softly as he sat on a bench, lowering his head into his hands. 'A cardiac unit? Is it the baby or Sally? One minute everything was going along so well—the next, our world just seemed to crumble.'

'Try not to worry, Selwyn,' Sam said with more confidence than Paula felt. 'Sally and the baby are in good hands.'

Just then, a doctor appeared accompanied by a nurse. He introduced himself as the cardiologist and sat down beside them. 'Your wife has suffered a minor heart attack,' he told Selwyn gently. 'She is recovering, and at the moment the baby does not seem to have been affected.'

'Oh, God,' sighed Selwyn. 'I can't believe it. Will they be all right?'

The doctor looked towards Paula and Sam. 'We're doing everything we can—as I said, the coronary thrombosis was minor and there appears to be no severe damage to the heart muscle. We're running tests, but for now I'm afraid I can't tell you very much more.'

After repeating himself once more for Selwyn's benefit, the specialist agreed to Selwyn seeing Sally for a few moments. Left alone, Sam and Paula walked slowly along the corridor.

'I'll wait for Selwyn and drive him back,' Sam told her. 'You'd better get back to the surgery. Don't worry, I'll stay with him until he feels he can cope alone.'

Paula nodded, lifting her eyes to his face. 'There's always the risk of complications, isn't there?'

Sam shrugged, looking weary. 'Unfortunately, yes. We won't know the effect of the heart attack on the baby just yet either. It could be days—weeks, even. It's going to be a traumatic time for the Walkers.'

CHAPTER FIVE

KYLIE GRANT was in the last few weeks of her pregnancy, a healthy young woman of twenty-six, expecting twins. Her partner, Mark Freen, stood at the door of their flat at half past three in the morning, looking the picture of despair.

'Thank God you didn't take long.' He sighed as Paula walked over the threshold into the tiny flat over a shop in Struan. 'You must have flown here.'

She didn't tell him that only moments ago, in the very next street, she had comforted the widow of an old man who had passed away peacefully in his sleep. There had been little she could do but give emotional support to the woman, herself in her late eighties. The heart failure had not been unexpected at ninety-five, but even so Paula had rung their son who lived in Warwick and waited until he'd arrived.

In Kylie and Mark's case, Kylie was already wanting to push when Paula entered the bedroom.

'I've phoned the midwife,' Mark said worriedly, hovering by the bed. 'My car's out of action. Kylie said to phone you as well, Dr Harvie.'

Paula had met Kylie at the antenatal classes. She had realized from the outset that Kylie was a bit of a rebel. One of life's natural anarchists, outgoing and volatile, Kylie had been confronted with one or two hard knocks early on but she had found a good partner in her quiet carpenter, Mark. Now she lay in a profusion of bedclothes, panting heavily.

'When did you begin contractions, Kylie?' Paula

hurriedly took a maternity pack from her case, spreading out the contents.

'Not long ago—it was so quick. I'm not due for ten days—I thought it was just a tummy ache after the fruit I'd eaten.'

Paula issued Mark with instructions for towels and hot water and then rinsed her hands quickly and examined Kylie.

'Any moment now, one of them is going to crown. Push when I say, pant in between, OK? Just as you've learnt at the clinic.'

Kylie nodded, her face bathed in sweat as she gulped a moment's respite. Then the baby began to crown. He slipped into Paula's hands with a triumphant cry, and Mark, who was standing watching with towels in his hands, wobbled a bit.

'Sit down, Mark,' Paula told him, and with a faint groan he collapsed into an armchair.

Smiling, Paula turned back to Kylie who was entranced by the sight of her son in Paula's arms. Soon he was wrapped and lowered to Mum, just as Mark groggily began to try to get to his feet.

'Have a sip of water,' Paula told him, and nodded to the glass on the bedside table. 'Then come and see. You've a beautiful baby son.'

He nodded, stumbling to the bed. 'Sorry,' he mumbled. 'I wasn't much use.'

The two women giggled. 'Look, isn't he adorable, Mark?' Kylie presented the baby to him, just as another contraction began. 'Here, take him. . .oh, God, Dr Harvie. . .' Kylie wrinkled her face and clutched the bedclothes.

'Kylie, push very gently now. . .'

'I want to push hard.'

'No, just a few seconds more. . .' Paula saw the tiny tip of the head appear. She waited a few more seconds, encouraged Kylie to push again, and then a beautiful baby girl slipped into the world. She yelled far louder than her brother and began to scream vociferously to her captivated audience.

'Oh, it's a girl,' breathed Kylie. 'A boy and a girl.'

Paula stood back as the parents gazed upon their newly extended family. 'Congratulations, both of you.' She smiled. 'They were worth waiting for, weren't they?'

Mark nodded and stroked the wetness from his eyes, kneeling beside the bed as Kylie sheltered a baby in each arm. To everyone's surprise, he took their tiny hands in his and looked up at Kylie. 'Now you can't say no any more,' he said croakily. 'Kylie, will you marry me?'

Kylie almost burst into tears. Paula tried not to encroach on the intimate moment which brought a lump to her throat. She knew that Kylie had been married before and her husband had deserted her, having begun an affair within months of their marriage. Kylie had vowed she would never marry again, and even when she had discovered she was having twins had remained adamant on the subject.

It seemed Mark had different ideas. The pregnancy had come out of the blue, but he had been the one to set up home for them in the tiny flat, and would have married her on the spot if Kylie had agreed.

Paula didn't hear Kylie's reply, but she busied herself with attaching the clips to the cord and cutting it as the healthy placenta came neatly away. When Paula had finished clearing, she realized the mood was tense in the room, softened only by the babies who were quieter now.

'They're beautiful,' she said, running a finger under Jasmine's chin. 'Two lovely babies, Kylie.'

At that moment the midwife, Betty Hill, came in.

'Pipped to the post!' she exclaimed breathlessly. 'Oh, let's see the little darlings. . .'

Her arrival appeared to resolve the tension between Kylie and Mark, and Paula laid baby Jasmine on the bed to examine more fully. The midwife weighed them, a little over 2.9 kilos apiece, pronouncing George and Jasmine the perfect twins.

'All present and correct as far as I can tell,' Paula declared, lingering in the hope of being able to hold one of them. Kylie raised Jasmine and Paula gently took her.

At every birth, she steeled herself for the inevitable— the memory of Emily. Sometimes she managed without too much trouble, more often than not, she'd have a delayed reaction—a dream, a small depression, a heaviness.

She braced herself as she gazed down on the baby's beautiful face. She was going to be a lovely creature, like Kylie. Emily had been perfectly formed, too. . .

George roared in the background. 'He's not sucking,' Kylie complained anxiously. 'What am I doing wrong?'

'Like this,' Paula coaxed, giving Jasmine to Betty. She took the little head firmly and moved his lips against the nipple, encouraging open his tiny mouth which was too absorbed in bawling. As he tasted the nectar Paula pushed gently, and soon nothing could deter him from filling his hungry stomach.

Jasmine proved much easier to accommodate, and Kylie laughed. 'She doesn't need telling twice,' she giggled. 'Do you think I'll have enough?'

'They'll soon let you know if you haven't,' Betty observed. 'Now, Dr Harvie, any sutures?'

Paula nodded. 'Just a couple, I think.'

After the feed, Paula completed three sutures, in fact, advising Kylie to have salty baths to help heal the tears. Before she left, she had a couple of minutes alone with Kylie. 'I just can't do it, Dr Harvie,' Kylie confessed.

'I can't bring myself to say yes to Mark. And I know I should for the babies' sakes. I just have this terrible fear that what happened before will happen again.'

Mark, Paula was sure, would be a doting father, absolutely trustworthy, and would love his little family to distraction. But she could fully sympathize with Kylie's reluctance. The girl had been deeply affected when her husband had left her and she had suffered a breakdown.

'Give it a few weeks, Kylie,' Paula advised gently. 'Your hormones are probably crashing around inside you, not knowing what's hit them after a double delivery. Get yourself mobile and into a routine and then talk to Mark about it again. I think he was just very emotional today.' She giggled. 'Good job you had an armchair in the bedroom!'

Kylie giggled too, brightening instantly. 'Daft thing. He doesn't know if he's coming or going,' she said, unable to hide her pride.

'Oh, this is nothing yet,' Paula laughed. 'Just wait till he gets a few night feeds under his belt.'

Paula left the midwife to cope and said her goodbyes, realizing it was almost dawn. A lemon-coloured horizon sparkled through the trees. She swung her weary legs into the Polo, drove to the surgery which was nearer than home and crashed out in the rest room until she heard the first roar of the vacuum cleaner.

Paula made herself respectable for her nine o'clock surgery, repairing the damage of the night as best she could. The change of clothes she kept at work came in handy. In the cloakroom she washed, brushed her teeth, changed into the fresh pale green Laura Ashley summer dress and pinned up her hair in a tidy chignon. Adding a touch of lipstick and mascara, she told herself that four hours' sleep was enough for anyone to cope on—anyone worth their salt as a GP, anyway.

Asking one of the girls to pop out and buy her a

sandwich before surgery, she gulped a couple of coffees and browsed through her list before demolishing the snack.

Her first patient, a twenty-year-old unemployed male, described what sounded suspiciously like a hangover from the weekend and complained of general flu symptoms. Paula recommended he go to bed, drink plenty of fluids and take paracetamol until he felt better. He seemed to enjoy talking about his symptoms, and Paula wondered if she was about to have a second Valerie Curry added to her list. As he left he almost bumped into Sam who was about to knock at her door.

'How are you, Steven?' Sam enquired, looking at him with an eyebrow crooked.

'Oh, fine, thanks, Dr Carlile.' And off he flew.

Sam was smirking. 'What was it this time?' he asked, coming in and closing her door.

'I suspect much the same as the other five times this year.' Paula nodded to the computer. 'I'm new—and he decided to test me out. Am I right?'

Sam grinned. 'Well, not exactly. He's a strange lad, our Steven. He seems to like coming in for a chat, though I have to admit he presents all sorts of minor but quite legitimate complaints, usually from accidents on his bike or even burns or scalds. He's bright enough, but he becomes bored with his jobs as far as I can make out.'

'I gave him pretty bland advice.' She shrugged. 'I couldn't really find anything wrong with him other than after effects of an indulgent weekend or possibly flu.'

'Sensible move. Doubt we'll see him again for a bit, though. Busy night, I see?'

She nodded. 'Somewhat. Mr Lessing died in his sleep and Kylie Grant produced two healthy babies. A boy and a girl.'

He tilted his head and stared at her. Her heart seemed

to tilt under the stare of those brown eyes, but at least this time she could put it down to lack of sleep.

'Talking of babies—'

'Have you heard anything from Selwyn Walker?' Paula interrupted. She had just the smallest suspicion he was going to refer to the conversation they had had over Emily and, frankly, she wasn't up to going through it all again this morning. 'Is Sally still in the cardiology unit?'

He nodded. 'So far, yes.'

'Perhaps I'll ring them—if you've no objection?'

He shrugged. 'Be my guest.'

She sifted the papers on her desk. 'Well, I'd better let you go. . .'

He grinned. 'Is this a polite way of brushing me off? I thought we'd agreed to try to get to know each other a little better.'

She smiled. 'To be honest, I haven't had time to give us a thought.'

'I don't know whether that's a good sign or bad,' he muttered wryly.

'Does it have to be either?'

'Human nature being what it is, yes.' He smiled, and she realized she wouldn't ever quite get used to its warmth—a beam of unadulterated brightness which lit up his features and his eyes. 'There's just one more thing. . .'

She pulled a face. 'Surprise me.'

His eyes glittered teasingly. 'Harry Bamford. Had you forgotten?'

'Oh, no. But I thought you had.'

He chuckled softly. 'I've something I'd like you to see. Can you pop into the cottage this evening?'

She was intrigued. 'I'm assuming the invitation has some bearing on the case that we can't discuss here?'

'It has. Why else would I be asking?'

Why indeed? she scolded herself, blushing. 'I'm on call again tonight.' She hesitated. 'And I'm afraid if last night was anything to go by. . . What about Thursday?'

He nodded, still grinning at her. 'Thursday's fine. My day off this week. Can you make lunch?'

'You must be joking,' she snorted. 'Have you seen the lists?'

He grinned as he turned to the door. 'On your way home, then. Whatever. I'll be there.'

'Sam. . .' she called as he opened it.

'You're going to change your mind,' he guessed, quirking an eyebrow.

She let out a sigh and lifted her shoulders. 'I was. . .'

'Don't,' he said with a wicked grin. 'You won't be disappointed, I promise.'

But on Thursday, after a day which had begun and ended with recalcitrant patients, she felt more like a wrung-out rag than a human being and began having dreams of slipping into a bath, staying there until her muscles unlocked and her head stopped throbbing, then falling into bed for an eternity of sleep.

In fact, it was a quarter to eight by the time she had finished at the surgery. She arrived on Sam's doorstep tense and tired, wishing she had time to change from the navy skirt and blouse she had worn to work.

'Hi!' Sam said as he opened the door. 'I thought you'd forgotten.'

She shook her head, staring at his fresh ivory shirt and cool cream trousers. The muted colours showed up his heart-stopping tan, his black hair folded back with care across his head enhancing the depth of his brown eyes.

'I'm sorry I'm late,' she said, feeling rattled and about as friendly as a porcupine, distinctly disadvantaged in her working clothes. 'It was bedlam at the surgery practically all day. And of all things we had to call the police tonight.'

'The police?' He gestured for her to enter. 'Come in—what happened?'

She followed him along to the kitchen. 'Well, I had Valerie Curry for at least half an hour this morning, setting me four patients behind, then Steven Crane came back to see me—'

'Surely not?'

'With a fractured wrist. A real one, which had to be X-rayed, but, of course, he didn't have a car or any money to go to Warwick.'

'So you ended up paying for a taxi?' he ventured sitting her down at the table in the kitchen.

'He's done the same with you?'

'Oh, yes. I think we've all been caught at some point.'

She sighed, shuddering at the recollection of her next patient, a woman who had been utterly over the top through drug abuse. 'Then I had a temporary resident in during the afternoon who had a medical history of nervous trouble, as she put it, and demanded a benzo-diazipine which I simply wasn't prepared to give her. I'm afraid there was an all-out argument, and she burst into Ken's room whilst he was in consultation with a patient. It took both Ken and I to restrain her from fighting with the patient, who just happened to be sitting there minding her own business and chatting to Ken. In the end, we were forced to call the police because she bolted herself in the loo.'

Sam tried to hide a smile. 'Did they persuade her out?'

Paula sighed. 'Eventually. By which time we were all nervous wrecks. I could cheerfully have swallowed a sedative myself!'

He leaned against the sink and folded brown arms across his chest. 'So you aren't terribly impressed with rural practice?'

She snorted. 'My eyes have been fully opened! In the city, drugs were a regular occurrence, one almost expected it. But here you sort of get lulled into a false sense of tranquillity—I suppose today just shook me a little.'

'Then let me help you unwind.' He turned to a bottle of wine that was unopened, plunged in a corkscrew, captured the bottle between his knees to pull the cook and poured a fraction into a glass. 'Just a sip. Doctor's orders.'

She took it and sipped obediently. 'Mmm. Delicious. But no more. I'm driving.'

Just as she lowered the glass to the table, an alarm went off behind her.

He leapt to the Aga, crouching down to peer at the oven. 'Timer's on the blink; better check, though.'

She almost fainted at the smell that flooded into the kitchen as he prodded at the contents of the oven with a spoon.

'Mixed herbs. . .?' she murmured, closing her eyes. 'Dill? Parsley?'

'Salmon bake,' he told her, retrieving a sumptuous pink fish from the depths of the Aga. 'Cooked in white wine and cream.'

'Not the sort of salmon that comes from the supermarket I go to,' she sighed as her stomach gurgled noisily.

'Then try the fishmonger. Preferably the one in Struan. On market days he lowers his prices to compete.'

Smiling, she watched him baste the fish and return it to the oven. 'Somehow, I didn't imagine you cooked.' She sighed.

He grinned. 'That's what comes from, to quote, "standardizing in a conventional form without individuality", unquote.'

'Stereotyping?' she guessed.

'Am I really like him?' He turned and drew his brows together as he stared at her. 'Your husband—are there really so many similarities between us?'

Her breath caught in her throat. She shook her head slowly. 'No, no, I don't think so.'

He stared at her, considering. 'That's not a very reassuring answer.'

Her heart in her mouth, she shook her head. 'You caught me by surprise. Am I like her?'

He leaned back against the sink and her heart seemed to be perched somewhere between her tummy and her throat. 'You're the same age,' he told her, 'the same confidence—the same career orientation.'

'Hard-hearted career women,' she murmured. 'Isn't that what you said?'

He stared at her. 'I hope I'm wrong.'

So now she knew, she thought as she took a breath, surprised at the odd sensation of tightening around her ribs. 'Appearances can be deceiving. It's unfair to generalize.'

He nodded slowly. 'It's not easy to be objective, is it? When you've been hurt, you wonder if it will happen again—you begin to wonder if you'll ever feel human again. And everyone else poses a threat. . .relationships are never the same. . .'

For a moment, as his words trailed away, the silence enclosed them. She took a swift sip of her drink and shrugged, replacing it on the table. 'I don't think I should drink any more,' she murmured. 'I'm not a very informed authority on relationships. Jay was the one man in my life. . .' She blushed, aware she had given herself away.

'You haven't thought of getting married again?' he began hesitantly.

She thought of the last five years and of the long and lonely climb back to recovery after her betrayal by Jay, culminating in the loss of Emily. Her trust had been shattered in everything but the belief that she alone had to forge a new life for herself. Allowing anyone to get remotely close would endanger her slow and painful return to recovery. Trying to find the humanity within her again hadn't been easy, still wasn't easy. The frightening thought was, in striving for survival she had become almost a machine, throwing everything—every ounce of strength and determination—into her work.

She looked down at her folded hands. 'No. I couldn't bear. . .' She felt as though she'd drunk a bottle of wine, not a few sips as she looked slowly up into his eyes. 'I don't think I can come to terms with the fear of losing another baby,' she found herself admitting.

'But the chances of the same happening again are limited. If there's nothing physically wrong. . .'

She put her hand up to her lips to stop them shaking, but a small sob escaped before she could control herself. Suddenly she was in his arms, his big hand pressing her head on his chest, her silent tears falling on the clean cotton of his shirt. 'I. . .I'm sorry,' she mumbled as she tried to wipe away her tears. 'I. . . I've never said that before, never admitted to it—'

'Then it's not before time, honey,' he whispered, holding her in his arms, gently massaging her hair under his fingers. 'You're facing the loss of Emily and your own fears. That's never easy for any of us. But fears are better shared, brought out into the open.'

She leaned her head heavily on his chest, closing her eyes, her fingers involuntarily gripping his solid body for comfort. 'I. . .I feel such a fool,' she mumbled. 'I should be over it.'

'There's no set time for recovery,' he said quietly above her. 'And it's good to weep, to set the emotions free.'

She could have stayed all night in the warmth of his

strong arms, just listening to the deep, generous throb of his speech rumble through the broad chest under her cheek, but she knew that way danger lurked and self-consciously she began to lift her head. He captured it between his hands, bending down to kiss each wet eye, and she felt him take out a handkerchief and wipe the tears from her face very gently.

She dredged up a smile from somewhere. 'Thanks,' she gulped. 'Thank you for listening.'

He stared into her eyes, searching them until a small smile trickled over his lips. 'Hungry?' he asked.

Suddenly she realized she was ravenous. 'Are you seriously inviting me to eat with you?' she said.

'I seriously am. Want to wash and brush up?'

She sighed. 'I'd love it.'

'Choice is yours. Bathroom's up the stairs and second on the left. The loo's downstairs, straight along the corridor. Supper's in ten minutes.'

She left him to it and went to discover the bathroom. Raiding the contents of her cosmetic bag, she washed, applied fresh lipstick and combed her hair into a silky bob, setting it free from the restraining pins. The headache seemed to have vanished, and the fact that she had revealed her fears seemed to have helped rather than hindered her equilibrium. There was a small light in her eyes which had not been there before—perhaps he was right and admitting to one's most intimate concerns was a step in the right direction. She just hoped she would feel the same tomorrow when she had to look him in the face on a professional level.

Glancing around the bathroom, she saw a pretty, egg-timer-shaped bottle with a golden bow clipped to its neck. She picked it up and sniffed it.

Who? she wondered, followed predictably by where and when? Jilly Cameron? In this house? Recently?

Unable to resist a last glance at the shelf, she discovered a couple of ambiguous deodorants that could be used by male or female. Expensive and half-used. . .

'Feeling better?' he said as she entered the kitchen later.

She went scarlet. 'I'm sorry about that. I don't know what came over me.'

'You're welcome—any time.' His eyes met hers for a moment before he nodded to a tray with two steaming plates of food on it. 'Let's eat.'

She followed him through the narrow hall into the dining room. The table had been marvellously set, including—surprisingly—pink napkins.

'Do you like asparagus?'

She nodded. 'I love it.'

'Help yourself.' He passed her the dish of buttered asparagus and then the salmon. He asked her more about what had happened at the surgery. 'Come on.' He grinned. 'Eat up.'

She did.

'Now for my surprise,' he said as they finished the meal with an exotic concoction of fruit salad and cream. He flicked on the video as he cleared the plates. She gazed abstractedly at the TV in the corner, and Harry Bamford lumbered across the screen. Harry turned sideways to the camera and tried to sit in a garden deckchair—which he couldn't—which was a relief because Paula could have seen the chair collapsing underneath him.

'Now,' said Sam enthusiastically, propelling her to the sofa. 'Watch.'

The screen went blank and Harry appeared again. This time, Harry lowered himself completely into the chair.

'He's lost weight,' Paula gasped, her eyes growing wide. 'He must have, to be able to squeeze into a deckchair!'

'Correct,' agreed Sam as Harry sat in the deckchair

and crossed his legs—something he told Paula he'd
never been able to do.

'But how?' Paula gulped.

'Look again and you'll see.'

'Mabel!' she exclaimed as a young golden Labrador
hurled itself across the lawn and into Harry's arms.

'Not Mabel but Milo,' explained Sam. 'The reason for
Harry's new sylph-like self. Simple. Dog needs exercise.
Harry does, too.'

'But that's amazing,' gasped Paula, staring at the
paused picture of Milo and Harry.

'I must admit I cheated a bit,' Sam confessed, sprawl-
ing beside her. 'Harry lived with his mother before she
died. They had an old mongrel they doted on. I took a
gamble that when Harry saw Milo he'd be hooked. Holly
said I could take Milo back if it didn't work out. But I
rather think it's been love at first sight.'

Paula lifted her eyebrows. 'I'm amazed—truly.'

'Harry's lost a stone and a half for starters.'

Paula stared at the screen. 'He looks so different.'

'He is different.'

She sighed. 'I just hope he keeps losing the weight.'

'Bound to, if he keeps the dog.'

'And the slimming group.' She looked at him under
her lashes. 'He's still attending, isn't he?'

Sam shrugged. 'Doesn't need to.'

'Do you mean you discouraged him?'

'He never cared for it—what was the point?'

She gaped at him. 'He told you so?'

'Not in so many words, but it was obvious he wasn't
getting anywhere, trudging along each week to a class
brimming with skinny women who made him feel useless because he didn't manage to lose a few pounds.
That's why your treatment didn't work. He felt intimi-
dated rather than encouraged, being pushed into
a group.'

'But Harry needs contact with other people,' she protested. 'He needs support. It's fine giving him a dog to walk, but what happens when the novelty wears off?'

He shrugged. 'It won't. Anyway, a man's outlook to a woman's is totally different when it comes to appearance. Why do women want to get thin? Why do women want to change their appearance? To attract a male, of course. Harry was like a fish out of water.'

Paula let out a breath. 'So much for enlightened male psychology!'

'It has its advantages.'

'None that are strikingly obvious,' she snorted.

'You,' he threw back at her pointedly, 'asked for my help and I gave it.'

'I just wish—'

'And I wish,' he interrupted, taking hold of her and drawing her into his arms, 'that you'd stop trying to climb onto that high horse of yours and. . .let me. . .'

His mouth came down to cover hers in a kiss which made her gulp back the words in her throat. When shock had completely annihilated every reasonable thought in her head, including any hope of resistance against his strength, she gave up the momentary struggle and melted against him, breast to chest, heart to heart.

Her lips moved against the soft stubble of his chin and he nuzzled a soft trail of kisses over her face, holding her head between his hands. 'Don't let's quarrel,' he whispered.

'W. . .we're not quarrelling, we were just. . .'

A shuddering sigh went through him, answered by her own.

'Paula, you're such a beautiful woman. . .'

Her hand lay flat against his chest, and under the thin cotton of his shirt she could feel the springy dark hair against her palm. Gradually her heart slowed and she stopped resisting him. He must have felt it, because he relaxed his grip, knowing she would not move away. He was silent, staring into her eyes, his breath teasing her hair as he drew his fingers slowly through its silky strands.

She shivered. 'Oh, Sam,' she sighed, linking her hands behind his neck, and his lips came down again and teased her mouth gently.

'I could make you forget. . .' he whispered against her cheek. 'You and I knew from the start. . .but we both wanted to pretend it wasn't attraction.'

'Physical attraction,' she croaked, her skin tingling under his soft kisses.

'But it's more than that now. You know it is.' He rubbed his thumbpads across her cheeks in a smooth, sensual, circular motion, tipping her chin up so their eyes met.

'Sam, I. . .I just don't feel ready. . .'

But even as she spoke those words he began to kiss her again, and she knew that her reluctance to let him begin to make love to her had only fuelled their desire, not quenched it.

CHAPTER SIX

'HUSH,' Sam whispered as Paula began to protest, brushing his lips briefly across hers. She trembled at the touch of his fingers on her flesh, fingers that had already begun to remove her blouse as he eased the thin straps from her shoulders, peeling them away from her skin, allowing the delicate silk garment to flutter to the floor. He leaned to kiss the small prominent bones at her throat, her eyes closing as his mouth travelled in erotic passage, making small pauses as he kissed and nibbled so teasingly, with no word of her protest from her.

He traced the soft outline of her shoulders, his fingers creating a cocktail of desire and delight that seemed to spill into her veins and pulsate throughout her body.

'I don't want to talk about anything but us,' he whispered, laying her gently back onto the cushions and deepening his kiss, fluttering his lips against her temple in a mesmeric cascade of small, deliberate kisses which left her faint with longing.

'S. . . Sam, no,' she protested weakly. 'This is crazy.'

'It certainly is not,' he murmured against her ear. 'It's perfectly acceptable behaviour between two people who are irresistibly attracted to one another.' His fingers curled over her mouth to stop her protest as he unclipped her bra with skilful gentleness, before he leaned down to attend to the small pink buds which rose at his demand, her body wanting him, demanding its own surrender to a greater power, an inevitability that seemed part and parcel of their relationship.

'You take my breath away,' he whispered, drawing her into the heat of his own body which seemed suddenly to be laying alongside her, half-naked. His brown torso was hard and muscular against her paler skin. The contrast of it made her gasp as she flicked her eyes over his half-clothed body, her breasts pressed wantonly against the dark forest of curling hair. Her small voice of warning seemed to be powerless now. She hardly heard it. Her desire was overcoming all else as he began to release the clip of her skirt.

'Oh, Sam,' she murmured helplessly, 'you've said it yourself—this is just something very physical. . .' It should have been so easy to let herself go, to surrender to the male dominance of his wonderful body and stop protesting, to be carried through on a wave of arousal that she had never experienced before. But it wasn't. The very selfish fear of becoming pregnant because of what had happened to Emily was still too vivid in her mind. 'Sam,' she murmured bleakly, closing her eyes, 'this is a mistake. . .'

He held her close, leaning to kiss her small, perfectly formed breasts and the still aroused peaks of desire which were contradicting all she was saying. Sensuously he began to make love to her, knowing instinctively, it seemed, what to do to delight and tempt her beyond bearing.

With senses swimming, she trembled in his arms, her response teetering on the edge of acquiescence, her lips opening for the taste of his, his skin moving against her own, leaving her bemused and weak. Only then did she realize she must stop him—only when her mind repeatedly drew her back to Emily, her ghost flitting achingly through her imagination, did she manage to push her fingers against his hard chest, flicking open her eyes to stare up at him with such sadness written in them, he stopped kissing her.

'No, Sam,' she whispered. 'It wouldn't be fair.'

'I'm willing to risk a little unfairness,' he muttered,

his hot body only inches away. She could even imagine she felt his heartbeat from this distance, felt its power and resonance.

'I don't,' she said quietly, 'expect you to understand. . .'

Tight lines of tension sprung sharply around his mouth, his ragged breathing brought under control by an effort of will that must have cost him dearly. He leaned back against the cushion, his dark hair ruffled against the brocade. Then as he gazed into her face, his eyes travelling from one feature to another, he shrugged.

'You're right,' he muttered. 'But I don't suppose you envisaged walking into the lion's den either this evening.' Only the pounding of her heart seemed to reach her ears as she scrambled self-consciously for her clothes. 'You don't have to rush off like a scalded cat, though. Stay,' he said in a persuasively soft tone as she slipped on her shoes. 'You can sleep in the guest bedroom. It's too late to go home tonight.'

She turned slowly, her heart wanting to agree but her mind knowing exactly what would happen if she did. 'I can't,' she murmured. 'Aunt Steph would worry if she didn't see the Polo there in the morning.'

'That's a poor excuse,' he reproved, his eyes lingering on her as she tried quickly to tuck in her dishevelled blouse.

'But it's the only one I have,' she admitted, going red. 'I must go, Sam.'

She stood uncertainly for a moment, before she reached to the coffee table and grabbed her bag as his dark eyes followed her reproachfully. She swallowed on the words she was trying to dredge up to say she was sorry. Instead, like an adolescent, she murmured goodnight, not meeting his eyes, and fled to the car.

*   *   *

Paula tried not to think of Candle Cottage last night.

She dressed for the last day of the week in a slim oatmeal-coloured linen suit and high heels. Just in case when she came face to face with him she suddenly had an overwhelming urge to crawl into the nearest cupboard, the knowledge that she looked reasonably presentable might give her an added degree of confidence.

Confidence which had been partially eroded by the realization that last night she had been forced to confront her past—and had not won. She was still vulnerable, still hurting. But that had still not stopped her body from responding to Sam. So why resist? Why put up so much of a fight when all the chemical reactions had been there?

She'd thrashed it over in her mind until sleep had reluctantly come at three in the morning. Then she'd dreamt about him—he and Jay seeming to be one person, their smiles intertwining, reaching out to her, telling her it was safe to walk towards them. Then she had been slipping…slipping into the mud of the riverbank, the water seeping up over her as she'd screamed for help, reaching for a branch which had suddenly metamorphosed into a tiny perfume bottle and begun to sink with her…

She'd woken up with a cry on her lips, bathed in sweat, trembling from head to foot, her heart pulsing in her ears.

The dream was still with her as she tried to concentrate on the paperwork stacked on her desk. The phone began its shrill bleating and she picked it up to hear Tricia's voice.

'Dr Harvie, I'll be quick. I have a call from Delhi on line two. The person on the other end, a Dr Singh from the Children's Memorial Hospital, is insistent he speaks to Dr Carlile or Dr Cameron. I've tried to explain I don't

know a Dr Cameron and Dr Carlile hasn't arrived. . .but
it's a dreadful connection. . .'

'Put Dr Singh through, Tricia.' Paula grabbed a pen
and pad. 'I'll see what I can do. When will Dr
Carlile be in?'

'His surgery's at nine. About half an hour, I suppose.'

'OK. Leave it with me.'

Tricia made the connection and Paula frowned at the
interference on the line. Finally Dr Singh announced
himself, though in rather scrambled English.

'If you can leave a message with me, I'll see he rings
you directly back,' Paula promised.

Dr Singh rattled off his message and Paula jotted
down as much as she could recognize of plain English.
She was staring bleakly at her note when Sam knocked
on her door ten minutes later. He looked devastating,
of course—she'd known he would. He was wearing a
crisp summer white shirt and dark trousers, and his hair,
as black as a raven, was brushed back. Brooding brown
eyes gazed down on her under their heavy lids.

She was becoming aware of the symptoms of her
body when she clapped eyes on him; a dangerously
arrested heart beat and then beating at a full gallop, heat
suffusing up from her toes to her neck. She was, she
supposed, quite capable of collapsing into a tangled
wreck if it hadn't been for the fact that common sense
told her that, even after what had happened at the
cottage, he seemed to be thankfully oblivious to the
emotional catastrophe he was inducing inside her.

Paula smiled up at him, her heart stubbornly beating
a tattoo into her throat until she'd forced it back into
place. 'You'd better come in—or are you going to
broadcast to the whole world?' she endeavored to joke.

He shrugged, closing the door behind him. 'I doubt
many people would be interested. We didn't get up to
much, did we?'

'I think you had better have this,' she said before she was forced to meet the deep irises which gazed at her. She passed him the note. 'I spoke to Dr Singh ringing from Delhi about ten minutes ago. I think most of it's accurate, though we had a horrendous line.'

He took the note and read it. When he looked up, he nodded slowly. 'It seems the funding's going through.'

'Congratulations, Sam.'

'I'm not counting my chickens—yet.'

Paula averted her eyes because she didn't want him to see what was going on in them, and at that moment she couldn't trust herself to speak.

'If—*if* we get the sponsorship from Lorimar Pharmaceuticals,' he told her, 'it'll mean we'll be guaranteed another ten years of specialist paediatric medicine for the unit. Otherwise—'

'The unit would have to close?'

'Unless someone else came up with finance. Maybe not a drugs house, perhaps a big soft drinks company or clothes conglomerate who need the media attention.'

'And you'll be returning—' Paula summoned her courage '—with Jilly Cameron?'

He looked at her curiously. 'Has she rung?'

She lifted her brows and shrugged. 'No—not as far as I know. It's just that Dr Singh wanted to speak to you or your partner, Dr Jilly Cameron. I just assumed. . .'

He glanced at the note in his hands. 'Jilly's been unavailable of late. Somehow I'll have to reach her.'

Just then Tricia knocked on the door and popped her head around. 'I'm sorry to interrupt, but we've an overflowing waiting room. Any offers?'

Sam swivelled around. 'Yes, send my first one in, Tricia.'

'Me, too,' said Paula, realizing the moment to discover more about Jilly Cameron was now lost. Still, what did it matter? She knew enough now to read between the lines.

Valerie Curry, her first patient, nurtured a fairly substantial chest infection and the prescription for antibiotic that Paula felt justified in giving was hurried away to the local chemist.

The viral complaints took precedence throughout the morning, along with sore throats and coughs and summer colds. Paula recognized the onset of what looked like a mini-epidemic for which she could do little more than advise bed rest, paracetamol and fluid. Ken and Sue had much the same impression as, at lunch time, they sat in the garden and ate, recalling some of the flu victims during the morning.

As John was on call and Sam was on a visit they demolished one of Sue's microwaved baguettes in relative peace. Paula was tempted to bring up Jilly Cameron and Dr Singh, but she had no need. Ken did it for her.

'If Sam decides to go back before Christmas,' he said, munching on a crispy roll in the shade of the gazebo, 'we'll need another locum. Shall I look around now, do you think?'

Sue was sitting on the swing seat with her feet up, Mabel dozing over them. Paula thought she looked less tired, but her ankles were still badly swollen under Mabel's golden paws. 'Let's wait until Sam knows a bit more,' she suggested. 'He's ringing Jilly this afternoon. They're meeting up to discuss things.'

Ken raised his eyebrows. 'Are they, now?'

Sue glanced at Paula. 'Has Sam mentioned Jilly to you yet?'

Paula said he had, briefly—and tried to feign disinterest. The fact that she was morbidly fascinated in the subject, she was sure, was written in psychedelic ink across her forehead.

'Stood him up for someone else,' murmured Ken

absently. 'As soon as they came back from Delhi. If you ask me she winds him around her little finger when she's at a loose end. Haven't seen hide nor hair of her for months and then, bingo, up she pops. Still, a woman who looks like Jilly and with a brain to boot—'

'Ken!' Sue spluttered. 'You old gossip!'

Ken looked at her blankly. 'Did I say something?'

Sue laughed. 'Jump in at the deep end with boots on, go right ahead.'

Ken was silent, then he turned to Paula. 'Oh, dear. Have I. . .?'

Paula shook her head furiously. 'Sam's love life is of no interest to me,' she said far too quickly, too emphatically. And, when they both stared at her, she gulped and jumped to her feet. 'I'm going to get an early start with my calls, then I'll come back and help you out with surgery, Sue.'

'Don't rush, Paula.' Sue threw a black look at her husband and lifted Mabel from her feet. 'I might look a wreck but I'm feeling quite well, actually.'

'Built like an ox,' Ken observed rudely.

Sue clouted him. 'The next time you want sympathy, Ken Dunwoody, you can sing for it.' She smiled and glanced at Paula. 'Don't take any notice of Ken. He's a frustrated gossip columnist. Missed his vocation completely!'

But as Paula paid her first house call to a young boy with a bout of bronchitis she worried away at what Ken had inadvertently let slip. Jilly Cameron was not only beautiful, she was intelligent, too, and obviously Sam was still involved in some way.

As she listened to seven-year-old Damien Matthews' chest, which was as wheezy as a percolator, she began to build a picture in her mind of Jilly. Totally inaccurate, she suspected, but what did it matter? She just needed to torment herself a little more with the kind of woman who wielded power so cleverly over a man like Sam Carlile.

'I'll prescribe a week's course of Amoxil,' she told Damien's mum. 'No school, I'm afraid, until we see a little improvement. Plenty of fluids if he's not hungry, and I'll see you in a week's time, young man.'

She had just arrived home that evening and was sitting on the lawn with Aunt Steph, telling her about the call from Delhi that day, when a grey Mercedes pulled up and Sam Carlile strode down the garden path.

Aunt Steph waved. 'Dr Carlile. How nice to see you.'

Paula tried to tame the butterflies in her tummy and told herself to prepare for something she wasn't going to like.

'Am I interrupting?' He sank into the spare deck-chair Aunt Steph had rattled at him.

Paula smiled sweetly from the garden lounger. 'Would it make any difference if I said yes?'

Sam chuckled. 'As a matter of fact, no. I've come to ask a favour.'

Paula rolled her eyes. 'Now, why am I not surprised to hear that?'

'I'm sure we'll help if we can, Dr Carlile,' Aunt Steph offered eagerly. 'One lump or two?'

'One, thank you. This is rather nice.' He sat back with the cup of tea Aunt Steph had poured him, his eyes skimming Paula's long bare legs and slender ankles propped unceremoniously on cushions. He met her grey gaze.

She knew it. What was in this visit for Sam Carlile? That, of course, was the question. She read it in his eyes.

'Fire ahead,' Aunt Steph said encouragingly.

He smiled, and Paula knew it was *that* kind of smile. A smile geared to pave the way for whatever request he was going to make, which was going to be even more awkward to refuse than usual because her Aunt was totally and utterly captivated.

Still, there was a simple remedy. A little word consisting of two letters; no. All it took was the will-power to say it and a firm fixture of concentration on the blackbird that was hovering on a branch just behind his head.

'I don't know if Paula's told you about—'

'Delhi?' her aunt put in, and Paula flushed.

He nodded, smirking at Paula. 'Lorimar Pharmaceuticals want a meeting, and I have to go to London tomorrow to try to tie up a few of the loose ends.'

Like Jilly Cameron for one, thought Paula taking a gulp of her tea.

'I think it will take a couple of days, which means— and I know it's a bit of a cheek—there's my on call duty and my list. . .?—'

'And you'd like me to cover for you?' Paula supplied briskly.

Aunt Steph looked bewildered by her niece's abrupt tone. Paula stared icily at Sam. Why did he have to come here and ask in front of her aunt? She knew why. It put her in an impossible position—she couldn't refuse.

'I can, of course, contact the locum service. . .'

'But you'd rather not?'

He paused. 'I'd prefer it if it were you.'

Paula almost choked on her tea. 'You mean to say— you trust me?'

'Of course he does, darling,' Aunt Steph gasped. 'You're a wonderful doctor. Isn't she, Dr Carlile?'

He caught her gaze and the brown eyes flickered. 'Yes, she is.'

Only when it's convenient for you to say so, she thought spitefully. As now, in front of my aunt.

'The other problem is. . .' he went on, rubbing his chin. . .'Mabel.'

'Mabel?' both women chorused.

'She's almost house-trained—almost. She still chews a bit and she. . .ah. . .still sleeps in a chair in. . .ah. . . the bedroom. And she does need her walks. . .'

Paula knew what was coming. 'And so?' she prompted.

'Well, Sue's going to have her work cut out with one doctor less. . .I was wondering—if you could possibly house-sit for a couple of days? I can't ask you to have Mabel here—she'd chew everything in sight and, as I say, she's not quite house-trained yet.'

'You want me to housesit Candle Cottage? Paula repeated.

'Yes,' he shrugged. 'Do you think you could? I'm thinking of Sue, you see. I don't want to put any more pressure on her in her condition.'

Before Paula could take a breath Aunt Steph leaned forward and sighed. 'How thoughtful, Dr Carlile. How sweet. Oh, Paula would be delighted, I'm sure.'

'Aunt Steph!'

The older woman laughed softly and squeezed Paula's hand. 'Don't you worry about me, Paula. We've a bridge tournament next week, so I should hardly have seen you, anyway. You go right ahead.'

Paula sought frantically for a reasonable excuse. But Aunt Steph had just put paid to any she could think of. She glared at Sam, who sat back in his chair and returned her arrow of ice with a sliver of pure sunshine in a smile that had Aunt Steph totally fooled.

'I want you to know,' Paula said, folding her arms across her chest the following morning, 'I'm house-sitting under protest.'

'Protest acknowledged and logged.' Grinning, Sam lifted Mabel from the stone floor of the hall in Candle Cottage. 'Her food's labelled in the freezer. The water turn-off is under the sink. The front door key is on the kitchen table and the back door one is jammed in the lock so you'll have to bolt it at nights...and I wish I were staying to keep you company,' he added, his voice sliding down her spine like cream.

Paula folded Mabel into her arms, nuzzling her face into the silky golden head to hide the outward signs of her treacherous heart yearning to say she did too. 'When do you suppose you'll be back?' she asked cautiously.

'Tuesday- ish? I'll ring you.'

Why should he bother to ring when he hadn't said where he was staying, hadn't left a number where he could be reached? Of course, she knew why. Jilly Cameron would probably have objected to a flood of phone calls gumming up her private line.

What am I doing to myself? she asked in silent reproach. I'm crazy even thinking about Jilly Cameron in this equation. Struan House Surgery is one doctor less, there's a puppy to be cared for and a colleague's workload to contend with—end of story.

She walked with him to the garden, let Mabel loose on the lawn and watched him open the boot and throw in his case. He turned towards her and their eyes met. In a moment of hesitation he stepped towards her, but the moment passed and he jumped into the car. Paula was left staring after him as he touched the horn and disappeared along the lane.

She was on call tonight and tomorrow.

Until then, she had three hours of undiluted peace. Idly she peeked around the cottage. The guest bedroom which he'd made up for her was tasseled and chintzy. His bedroom she ignored completely, save to glance around for photos of which there were remarkably few. There were two. One of his parents, possibly in their seventies, she guessed, parents of whom Sue had told her a little. They had died several years back. Sam had come from a medical background, mother and father both doctors who'd had practices in Northumberland. The second photo looked like an older brother, a vet who had emigrated to New Zealand. The family resemblance was strong.

Paula gazed at the faces for a while, knowing these were the kind of people who provided a secure background. Sam and his brother had been fortunate—and then, with a small sigh, she reminded herself that Aunt Steph had provided her with all the love and support she had missed from parents.

Dragging her eyes away, she was shocked to discover she was relieved as she hurried from the room. No reminders of Jilly Cameron—not until she arrived downstairs.

In the front room, she was met with a library full of videos. The camcorder lay on a table beneath—was this where she would find the key to Sam's past?

She ignored the immediate wash of guilt at snooping and told herself he would have had the videos under lock and key if he didn't want them played. She walked slowly over, bent down and began to examine the labels.

Three cups of coffee later, snuggled on the sofa with Mabel lying across her feet, Paula clipped off her third video. The last video had given her a jolt, as her own face had materialized on the TV screen. She had looked completely staggered at the camera and then smiled with such a painful effort that she had closed her eyes, unable to watch her clumsy and startled movements.

If only she had been prepared for that first onslaught she might have responded with a little grace and dignity. Sue must have seen it because of Poppy's party.

Poppy looked adorable in her pink party frock, and Sue had looked so much better herself. But then, that had been towards the beginning of the pregnancy. Now she would be what. . . Paula did a sum in her mind. . .

six months? With the strain of still working and looking after Poppy and Ken was the pressure becoming too much? She determined to talk to Sue whenever she could find the right moment.

The fourth video was marked simply, 'Delhi'. Paula had been saving it. She plumped Mabel in front of her food in the kitchen, checked her watch and made a ham sandwich and another coffee. At half six she would be on call. Time enough to watch the video and eat the snack on her lap.

Curled on the sofa once more, she pressed the video button. Another world appeared before her eyes.

The following Tuesday Sam's voice came over a very indistinct line. 'How's Mabel?'

'Fine.'

'No problems?'

'No, none.'

'How's the cottage?'

'Fine.' How did he expect it to be? Demolished? Burgled? Repainted?

A pause which she was determined not to fill.

'Are my patients missing me?'

'Not a bit. As a matter of fact, I've Mrs Jessop waiting. . .' She was determined not to ask about London, Lorimar or Jilly Cameron—two whole days had passed without one phone call. So much for his promise to ring! She knew enough about Jilly Cameron to know why he hadn't.

Images immediately flashed up in her mind from the video. Extreme poverty and human strife spilling into the streets and, amidst all this, saris of the brightest, most exotic colours,—reds, yellows and purples—, women with eyes like jewels glimmering out under their dark hair. The hospital built in pure white stone and the pathetic faces of children looking into the camera lens from their beds. Some, starved and disease-ridden, lying in possibly the cleanest sheets they would see in the whole of their lives. Others able to sit and watch what was going on, their arms and legs as thin as matchsticks.

And in the middle of the film a Western doctor, smiling up at the camera serenely, a woman with intelligent dark eyes and auburn hair coiled into a knot above her white coat. She sat at a desk but neither the plain office setting nor the simple surroundings could detract from the beauty that Paula had, for moments, been hypnotized by.

She'd been sure it was Jilly Cameron. There had been no other Western doctor on the video and as she'd replayed it several times she'd became convinced it was.

'Paula. . .' he was saying, and her heart began to sink as she sensed what was coming. 'Do you think you could possibly cover for me until Thursday?'

'Thursday?' she repeated in astonishment.

'I'm having problems this end. It seems I'll need a couple of days longer than I thought. . .'

She could guess the kind of problems he was having and it wasn't to do with Lorimar, she was sure!

Then Mrs Jessop came in. Paula mumbled something ambiguous to Sam, annoyed with herself for sounding so petty. What was wrong with her? Was it so objectionable, living in Candle Cottage, for heaven's sake?

She was forced to admit, not at all. Despite the fact it had been a busy on-call weekend with the flu epidemic, she'd worked for an hour in the garden on Sunday afternoon. Mrs Next Door had made her a cup of tea and passed it over the hedge. Not that she'd done anything to warrant it—just weeded the nearest border for some exercise both mentally and physically.

Her nights had been broken by calls from the elderly mostly. Nausea, aching limbs and temperatures had followed the usual pattern. She'd written prescriptions

for paracetamol and Dioralyte and given a shoulder to
lean on to those who'd needed someone to talk to in
the early hours.

Mrs Jessop had been one of these. A widow and
desperately alone, she had found the flu hard to cope
with and at four a.m. on Sunday morning had called the
doctor. It had been five o'clock by the time Paula had
fallen back into bed after managing to convince Mrs
Jessop that rest, paracetamol and plenty of fluids was
the only advice she could give her.

'I still feel groggy,' Mrs Jessop complained now,
looking as white as a sheet.

Paula checked her thoroughly but there was nothing
she could find other than a severe case of stubborn
flu. She advised a return to the couch and a blanket if
not bed.

By the time Mrs Jessop had left, three similar cases
had accumulated in the waiting room. As she saw these,
Paula reminded herself to phone the hospital and ask
how Sally was.

Not that she ever managed to make the call. Five
minutes before the close of her evening surgery, Ken
Dunwoody rushed into her room. He was grey and shaking and he had trouble in getting out what he was
trying to say.

Eventually, he calmed himself. 'Paula, Sue's not too
bright, I'm afraid. I wonder if you'd come and see what
you think? The trouble is, she won't tell me exactly
how she's feeling—and, by the looks of her, it's not
too good.'

CHAPTER SEVEN

WHEN Paula and Ken rushed into the bedroom, there was no doubt in Paula's mind what was happening by the look on Sue's face. As Ken went to Sue, Paula grabbed the extension in the room and called an ambulance.

Sue was crying as Ken bent over her, brushing back her hair. 'I think I'm miscarrying,' she stammered. 'I had a small blood loss and I thought I'd wait to see. . .'

Ken turned to Paula. 'I should have had my way. I should have taken her in. I wanted to at lunch time. I knew she wasn't well.'

Paula put her hand on his arm. 'The ambulance will be here soon. Do you want to go down and tell the girls? And perhaps check with John that he's okay to take the on-call?'

He hesitated, the strain across his face contorting his normally placid features.

'I'll get Sue ready,' Paula encouraged. 'Try not to worry, Ken.'

After he had gone, Paula gently examined Sue, and her heart sank. The dark red blood loss indicated a haemorrhage, but she tried not to reveal how worried she was as she propped Sue more comfortably and helped her to changed her underwear, padding her with some absorbent towels.

'I'm going to lose the baby,' Sue said in a quiet voice.

Paula shook her head. 'You're not if I have anything to do with it. Now, take some deep breaths, Sue.'

Sue held her hand tightly. 'I'm scared, Paula. If the bleeding's coming from the placenta I might be all right,

111

but it'll mean a Caesarean if I'm haemorrhaging too much. Otherwise. . .' she paused to swallow her tears '. . .it's a D and C to clear the uterus.'

'Stop thinking like a doctor,' Paula said firmly as she disposed quietly of the stained sheet. 'And think like a mum-to-be. Talk to her—'

'Him,' said Sue stammeringly. 'I feel it's a boy.'

Paula squeezed her hand. 'Then tell him you love him and you'll bring him safely through.'

Sue looked up at her. 'Do you really think talking to him would make a difference?'

Paula could hardly tell her that when Emily had been born she had been in too much of a state of shock to try to communicate with the struggling little life inside her. But over the years she had wished fervently she had used some kind of internal language to communicate, to comfort her baby, to will her through to life.

'Yes, I do,' Paula said honestly. 'Now, I'm going to ask Mrs McDuff if she can organize Poppy and Mabel. Have you an overnight bag somewhere?'

Sue pointed to the wardrobe. 'It's all packed.'

Paula hauled it out, made sure Sue was comfortable and went downstairs to Mrs McDuff who was giving Poppy her supper. She told Paula not to worry about either Poppy or Mabel, and then within seconds the ambulance blared its way into the drive.

Ken went with Sue in the ambulance and, grabbing her bag from her room in surgery, Paula locked up again. The journey was swift, ten minutes along deserted roads which were luckily uncongested after tea time. Sue was admitted straight into Intensive Care and Ken and Paula were asked to wait in the lounge whilst she was assessed.

'She was haemorrhaging in the ambulance,' Ken choked as he tried to gather himself. 'Quite badly. She's lost a lot of blood. It was my fault I should have made her come in as soon as I suspected something. The trouble is, I'm so used to her being fit. The trouble with all doctors I suppose. You tend to take your wife for granted if she's a professional, too.' He wrung his hands. 'Damn it. I'll never take her for granted again.'

Paula tried to comfort him, but he paced the lounge until finally the attending physician came to talk to him. Ken came back to tell her that she was going into Theatre. 'I'm going with her whilst she's anaesthetized,' Ken said in a washed out voice. 'God knows if they'll let me stay. Why don't you make a move home? I'll let you know how it goes, Paula. You've done so much already.'

'I've no intention of going anywhere,' Paula told him kindly. 'I'm going to find myself a coffee and I'll make myself comfortable. If you want me, I'll be right here.'

He squeezed her hand, unable to reply, and with world-weary shoulders disappeared back into Intensive Care.

Paula settled herself down to wait.

She didn't know how long it was she waited, but it was dark when she next looked out of the window. Small speckles of light announced a busy car park and the arrival of visitors.

The lounge attached to Intensive Care was still empty and there was no sign of Ken. Paula shuddered, not with cold, but with empathy for Sue. She understood what she must have gone through this afternoon. Paula leaned her head against the glass, wishing there was something more constructive she could do. Suddenly a hand gripped her shoulder gently and she turned, staring up at the last person she'd ever expected to see.

'Sam,' she gasped incredulously, her grey eyes flying open. 'What are you doing here?'

'What do you think?' he said softly, his brow creased in a worried frown.

'But how did you know?'

'I rang you back this afternoon. John took the call and told me what was going on. I jumped in the car straight away. Thank God the M40 was clear and I managed to whistle home in no time.' He took her hand and, tugging her towards him, he kissed her hard on the mouth. 'I've missed you,' he whispered hoarsely.

'I'm glad you're here,' she managed in a shaky voice.

'So am I.'

She looked up into his dark eyes. 'But what about London?'

He shrugged. 'It can wait. What about a stiff coffee?'

Paula smiled. 'I'd love one.'

He tugged her towards the coffee machine and dropped several coins in the slot. Then he made her sit down with the drink, his big hands firmly planting her in a comfortable seat.

'You look terrible,' he said, sinking down beside her. 'Now, drink up and tell me what happened.'

Paula explained and he listened attentively to her, nodding occasionally. 'Has Sue had any spotting before today?' he asked, and Paula shook her head.

'I honestly don't know. But she's looked pretty shattered for days.'

'I wouldn't be surprised if she had and kept it to herself,' Sam muttered grimly. 'Not wanting to worry Ken—or any of us, come to that.'

Paula was inclined to agree. 'I wished I'd pressed her into relaxing more.'

'You've done your bit—more than enough. If I'd only given the situation a bit more thought I'd never have gone haring off to Lorimar.'

Or to Jilly Cameron, Paula found herself silently adding.

Just then the doors of Intensive Care opened and Ken appeared. His eyes were puffy and he wore a green protective gown which he was struggling to peel off.

Paula jumped to her feet, aware of Sam close beside her.

Ken staggered to a halt, his eyes wet with tears, and he took out a handkerchief and blew his nose vigorously. 'Sorry about this,' he apologized, not meeting their gaze. 'I'll be all right in a minute.'

'Take your time,' Sam said in his deep voice.

Ken nodded, drawing his hands over his face, not querying Sam's presence, even. 'They've given her a transfusion,' he told them. 'Had to. She lost a lot of blood.' His voice was barely audible as he looked up at them, and a smile trembled across his lips. 'But she's going to be all right.' And on a long, expelled breath broken by a half sob, he swallowed. 'We've a son— just five pounds. . .two and something kilograms, I think they said. And he's screaming his lungs out. He looks healthy—hands, head, feet, hips. Oh, God, I can't tell you the relief. . .'

Paula sat in Sam's Mercedes feeling as though she had just walked from John O'Groats to Land's End. Perhaps, emotionally, she had trudged a long way tonight. The last half an hour seemed to have sapped every drop of energy from her.

Ken had collapsed on the nearest seat. He'd started thinking about the amniocentesis and how he'd tried to pressure Sue into it. He hadn't been as confident, he now admitted, that he would have been able to cope with another disabled child—Sue hadn't been able to confide in him as she wanted.

Sam had reassured him that probably he was the last person Sue would have turned to if she hadn't been feeling well since she wouldn't have wanted to worry him. He wasn't a mind reader, so the odds were he could have done nothing to avert the haemorrhaging.

Paula had once again been grateful for Sam's presence and she'd made no protest when he'd suggested she leave her car keys with Ken since he'd come in the ambulance and they travel back to Struan in the Mercedes.

'Better relieve Mrs McDuff of Mabel,' Sam said as they neared the twinkling lights of the town. 'I'll pop in and pick her up and bring Mrs McDuff up to date.'

'Do you want me to come in with you?'

He shrugged in the darkness. 'I'll not be a few minutes. Then I'll get us home.'

It wasn't until after he had parked in the surgery car park that she realized exactly what he had said. She was almost dozing off with her head against the head rest when the word 'home' suddenly resounded in her brain.

Shooting upright in her seat, she blinked her tired eyes. Candle Cottage was home at the moment—all her clothes were there and her cosmetics, her shoes and her books. She'd left the place dishevelled as far as she could remember.

She was startled as Sam levered himself back into the car. Mabel squirmed herself into her lap, licking ferociously.

'Poppy's asleep,' he said, starting the engine. He handed her a Tupperware box which felt peculiarly warm. 'Mrs McDuff and Poppy cooked chicken and leek pies. Ken's got one in the oven and this is for us.'

'That's sweet of her.' Paula frowned hesitantly. 'But where do you propose we eat it?'

'The cottage, of course.'

She stared at him. 'You mean. . .I should stay at the cottage?'

'Why not?'

'Well. . .' she stammered. 'There's no need now.'

'Look,' he sighed, running a hand across the stubble of his chin and squinting into the darkened road. 'If you think you're in any danger staying the night, there's a three-and-half-inch bolt on your door and all you have to do is lock it. But to be perfectly frank, since I haven't had a good night's sleep recently, the thought of Mrs McDuff's chicken pie and an early night is more of an aphrodisiac to me than chasing you around the cottage until the early hours.'

'Sam, I wasn't suggesting—'

'Oh, yes, you were.' His voice was amused. 'And if you're worried about the neighbours, then you're worrying unnecessarily. They're a pretty broad-minded lot around here. I've had no complaints as yet.'

Paula stared at him. 'Oh, very reassuring!' She frowned back at the road. 'As it happens, I'm shattered, too.'

'In which case,' he murmured dryly, 'neither of us has anything to worry about, have we?'

Mabel lay on the sofa throw, snoring.

The chicken pie was vanquished and the bottle of wine Sam had produced from the pantry was three-quarters empty. The washing up lay in stacked piles on the drainer in the kitchen, and Paula sat in an old pair of jeans curled in a cavernously lumpy chair, her feet tucked up under her bottom and her head resting back on the mountain of cushions as Sam made his phone calls to London on the hall extension.

She couldn't hear him talking because he'd put on a CD. The soft, lilting music by Bach filtered around the cottage and, after her second glass of wine and the delicious pie and vegetables Mrs McDuff had supplied, she managed to close her eyes.

When Sam eventually came back in she didn't hear him. He must have been standing over her as she opened her eyes and gazed directly up at him.

'Sorry. . .did I disturb you?' He dug his hands in his pockets and moved away, finally opting for the comfy recliner opposite her. His tall body filled it amply as he eased into it, long legs stretched out as he struggled to loosen his tie, lifting his chin and snapping open the first two buttons of his shirt.

Paula stared at the dark hair growth running up into the brown well of his neck and rapidly she shook her head. 'No, I wasn't asleep. Did you manage all your calls?'

He shrugged. 'The guy I'm dealing with at Lorimar seems fairly certain we've secured the funding. I was supposed to finalize the deal in the morning, but he says he doesn't think there will be a hitch. . .'

Paula frowned. 'Is it so complicated to secure funding for such a worthwhile cause?'

'It is when you can't get hold of the people you're supposed to tie it up with.'

'And can't you?'

He gave her a grim smile. 'We need two signatures. Mine and Jilly's. Unfortunately. . .I simply can't get hold of her.'

'Does she live in London?' Paula ventured hesitantly.

'When she isn't orbiting around the planet, yes.'

Paula studied the lines of his face, which became hard and unforgiving as he stared down at the glass in his hand.

'She hurt you a lot, didn't she, Sam?' Paula whispered softly.

He looked up at her, his expression impassive except for the momentary flare in his dark eyes. 'We met in Delhi. We had the kind of relationship that never promised to work out—had I cared to take a good look at it. Jilly is devoted to climbing the professional ladder and woe betide anyone who gets in her way. I was just a rung—a lowly rung—with connections at the time. Delhi held its attraction for just about as long as I did. The potential Lorimar funding made headlines for a bit, then the novelty wore off when the spotlight transferred to the States.'

'America?' Paula frowned. 'Jilly's in America?'

He shrugged. 'She was—the last I heard—assisting Justin Delmont of the medical series fame.'

Paul's eyes widened. '*The* Justin Delmont?'

He gave a cynical little snort. 'She met him in Delhi— they'd come to shoot scenes for a couple of the episodes. He came to the hospital to ask for some help with the research for the filming. Research Jilly was more than happy to collaborate with—body and soul.'

Paula saw the hurt and anger flare again in his eyes. 'I'm sorry, Sam,' she sighed softly.

'Don't be. I was a fool—at the least.' He stared at her with liquid brown eyes, their lids partially shrouding the hurt beneath. 'When I was training, I lived with a girl—a woman. She was seven years older than me and I thought she was the most impressive person I had ever met. She was a lawyer. Her name was Abigail Charles and, I discovered, she was a most ambitious, independent lady, complete with charm and humour. I was besotted. She was clever and totally career oriented. Which was fine. As long as I remembered that, which I didn't. I asked her to marry me.'

He gave a sharp laugh. 'Tragic, wasn't it? A trainee asking a qualified professional female to marry him. But, you see, I thought she loved me. She said she loved me. The next day I came home and she'd moved out.'

For the first time since she had met him, Paula began fully to understand him. She was moved by his frank admission of the way he had been hurt, and she was just about to speak when he looked up at her with eyes which caught her heartstrings in a sharp and painful tug.

'You would have thought I'd have learned,' he went on in a self-mocking tone, 'but, five years later, I fell for exactly the same type of woman. Diana was at least

younger and less qualified than me, but she was a doctor.
I met her in the States when I was there for two years
with a specialist paediatric team. I decided to apply
for a consultancy with a paediatric clinic on the west
coast—'

He shrugged, a darkness edging his eyes as he seemed
to be lost in memory. 'And apparently so did she—after
"borrowing" the information for the job application from
my desk. One of the directors of the hospital was a very
rich man. Diana saw her opportunity and landed the job.
Not that I begrudged her the job in the end—I'd already
decided it was not right for me—it was just the fact she
moved in with him to get it.' He took a breath, inhaling
slowly, his mouth in a tight line.

'Ambition is a crazy thing. It drives people into
savage situations. I swore then I would never let it taint
my life again. Which is all the more absurd when you
think the next move I made was to India and. . .' he
stared down at the floor, his brow deeply creased. 'And
you know the rest of the story.'

She was stunned for a second. She shook her head,
wrapping her arms around her knees. 'I don't know what
to say, Sam—'

He looked up at her with a regretful smile. 'My love
life seems to pale into significance when I think of the
pain you must have been through with Emily. I never
really lost anyone I loved. Not like a daughter. That
must be the very worst of bereavements.'

She nodded, the old ache niggling at her ribs at the
mention of Emily, but this time she wanted to bring it
out into the open. This time it felt—safe. 'Emily was
just a perfect little girl,' she murmured softly, 'but without the gift of life. I. . .I sometimes think I took it away
from her. If I hadn't discovered Jay was having an
affair—if I'd been able to forgive—the shock might not
have been so great. She might have survived. . .'

'Do you really believe that?'

She shrugged. 'I don't know. Time is supposed to rationalize things. But Mum never came to terms with Dad leaving her just after I was born. Aunt Steph said she gave up when he didn't come back. She said Mum died of a broken heart—that it's perfectly possible. I think. . .I think I believed that. I think my heart broke when I found out about Jay's involvement.'

'And you think Emily's death was the result?'

Paula blinked, nodding. 'Perhaps. . .I don't know. I'll never know.'

He reached forward, took her hands and drew her across to slide into his lap. She went willingly, needing to be comforted, needing to exorcise Emily with some-one she trusted. 'I was thirty weeks,' she whispered into his chest. 'Emily was born by Caesarean section. She never breathed in this world, but I know. . .I feel. . .'

'She still lives?'

'I've always thought it was my imagination—her presence with me. But I discovered something about myself today. I told Sue to talk her baby through. . .to will him into life. She asked me if I really believed that. I said I did. And I do.'

'Let me in to help you,' he murmured against her ear. 'I won't hurt you. I want to see you happy—free from the past.'

But you will hurt me, Paula cried inside. Like Dad and Jay you'll leave me and I'll be alone again and dying of the pain of separation. I've survived twice—but I shan't a third time. There'll be nothing left to fight with, Sam, my love.

'Paula,' he whispered above her as though he could hear her thoughts, 'can you honestly say shutting out companionship is a way of life? Isn't it more a way of slowly dying? Don't we need one another to survive?'

She was shaking, she realized. He folded his fingers

gently around her upper arms. 'Jilly taught me a valuable lesson. She was committed to believing in herself. I didn't stand a chance. I wanted marriage, kids—the whole works. I felt I'd done my bit for others. And I thought Jilly would want England, a home, a family. . . it took me a while to find out what a fantasy I'd been living.'

She was trapped by the expression in his eyes as she stared up at him, and he wiped the wetness from her cheeks with his finger. Aunt Steph had been right. He was wounded—somewhere deep down. If he wasn't he wouldn't have been able to see into her emotions, know what she had been feeling today.

'There is. . .one more thing,' he said lifting his dark brows. 'I know we scare the hell out of one another, but haven't you realized—we need each other, too?'

She took a sharp, heady breath. It was happening now. Just as he had said. Her heart hurt—it was crying out to be healed—and there was a chemistry that churned and ached just beneath her breastbone, something that began when she was close to him. Or thought of him. Or touched him. But to acknowledge it. . .?

'I'm afraid, too,' he whispered, tilting up her chin so that he could stare into what felt like the depths of her soul. I'm afraid to want you. I'm afraid, because I've wanted before—' He took her face between his hands. 'I was wrong about tonight. I was wrong about you being safe. I was wrong to tell myself you were an ambitious creature who was too preoccupied with herself to notice what was going on in the world around her. I was wrong. And I apologize.'

The sensation of the pads of his thumbs gently smoothing a path to her ears—his heart beating wildly under hers—his smell, his feel, his vibration under her fingers, drawing her into zones that were mind-shatteringly unsafe. 'Sam,' she mumbled, shaking her head, 'just because we've talked about our pasts—'

'And are comforting one another—giving each other a little support as we might anyone who came to us asking for help. What's so very wrong with that?' His mouth skimmed her neck tantalizingly, smoothing across her ears and her cheeks with butterfly kisses and, finally, in swift possession he took her mouth, searching for her response which came swiftly, desperately, as she gave in to the pressure of his arms linked tightly around her.

'I want you, Paula, and I know you want me,' he whispered, breathing against her ear as she groped for breath. 'Let me in. I won't hurt you.'

She lifted her face, letting his kisses rain down on her, her mind numbed by his sweet words and the intimacies. And had not the shrill ring of the phone in the hall made them both jump and Sam's face fall in a dejected mixture of anger and surprise—if the noise had not be so heartlessly insistent—they might well have both chosen to ignore it.

But, knowing better than to be able to do so, Sam kissed her on the lips with a look which belied words and heaved himself wearily upward and away, the sound of his sigh lingering in the air, as did the scent of his aftershave, as a painful, poignant reminder of what might have been.

Whilst she heard the soft murmur of his voice, she found her hands automatically reaching to tidy herself, to cool her hot cheeks with her palms and to give one last deep breath of resignation as she too slowly rose to her feet. She knew before he re-entered the room that he had been called out, and she smiled knowingly as he came towards her.

'One of my patients from Westmead's nursing home, I'm afraid. He's an old chap of eighty-nine and in the last stages of cancer. I don't think he'll see the night out.'

'Westmead's? That's close to Aunt Steph's,' she whispered as he pulled her towards him, dropping a kiss on her forehead. 'You can take me home, after all.'

'Damn! I should have lied,' he said, closing his eyes. 'I must be tired.'

'I think we both are. It's probably best in the long run.'

'Speak for yourself,' he groaned, sighing deeply. 'Can't I persuade you to stay?'

She didn't want him to go—and yet she didn't want to stay—too much thinking could be done in his absence.

But as she climbed into the car and watched him tiredly assume the daunting responsibility of his terminal patient she was sure of the decision she had made.

But she had been almost—*almost*—tempted.

Sue's delivery of her baby boy was soon general news as Ken announced to the world the arrival of Jeremy Kenneth Dunwoody.

The week after Paula left Candle Cottage and returned home to Aunt Steph's, as if Jeremy had started a baby boom in the village, Sally's husband rang in from Warwick General to say they were considering taking Sally to Theatre. Selwyn Walker did not seem to know more, only that the baby was in distress.

Paula was alarmed by the news. Glancing at her watch, she gauged she had only one more patient to see and then she was free until three-thirty in the afternoon. 'Either Doctor Carlile or I will come,' Paula told him, and he seemed relieved.

She hesitated in phoning through to Sam. After the travesty of the night when she had so wanted him, yet rejected him again, it was still difficult talking to him as though nothing had happened. It wasn't Jay—it was the thought of all that pain waiting to happen once more in her life.

How could she trust Sam? How could she allow herself to fall in love again?

She couldn't risk a life she'd fought so hard to rebuild. . .

Just then, a young woman came into her room bringing with her her two month-old little girl for her DTP immunization. Paula cajoled herself instantly into workmode, pushing thoughts of Sam from her mind.

She effected the injection smoothly, and Cara crumpled her tiny face for a while which transformed into laughter when Paula wiggled her toes and made silly faces.

'The next one is in a month,' Paula reminded Mrs Jolly, who grimaced.

'I think I dread them more than she does,' she gulped.

'Oh, don't worry, most mums are the same,' Paula smiled as she walked them to the door.

'How's Dr Dunwoody's little boy?' Mrs Jolly enquired curiously. 'He was awfully early, wasn't he?'

'Early and healthy,' Paula took care to impress. She'd had several patients ask in a rather roundabout way how the baby was—and Paula understood the concerns of spina bifida or Down's, since everyone knew Poppy was a Down's child and that Sue had stuck out against amniocentesis.

It was a relief to be able to say Jeremy was a beautiful, healthy little boy, but sometimes she felt like adding that, even if he had been born handicapped, Ken and Sue would have loved him no less.

Paula saw off Mrs Jolly and made a snap decision to talk to Sam. She entered his room at the sound of his voice with only a fraction's hesitancy. He was up to his chin in paperwork and scraps were scattered from one extremity of his desk to the other.

'Don't ask,' he warned her grimly. 'I'm trying to dig up some notes I made on a referral to a specialist. My

fault. Should have put it straight onto computer.' He
tried to decipher a crumpled piece of paper, then thrust
it into the waste-paper basket. She studied him for a
moment, seeing his long brown artistic fingers, the same
fingers which had soothed and caressed her, run over
her skin like silk and travelled a tantalizing path over
her face, holding her still as he had kissed her.

Paula blinked, refusing to let herself be sidetracked.
'Sam, I've just heard from Selwyn Walker, Sally's
husband.'

His head shot up immediately. 'Is Sally OK?'

'Sally is—so far, but it's the baby. They've taken her
to Theatre.'

His face darkened. 'Damn.'

'I know, I'm worried, too. Look. . .' she nodded to
the catastrophe surrounding him '. . .you're busy, but I
think one of us should go. Sally's your patient, but I've
a couple of hours free before afternoon surgery. How
are you fixed?'

He sighed. 'Impossible. I've three waiting, two tacked
in as emergency appointments and at one I'm supposed
to have this done.'

'Are you happy with me going?' she asked hesitantly.

There was just a moment's hesitation before he
shrugged. 'I suppose there's no alternative.'

Not exactly the answer she'd hoped for, but what did
she expect? She knew how it felt to be trapped in surgery. And he'd obviously not had a good morning, which
must make not being able to see Sally in whose case he
was deeply involved all the more frustrating.

'Tell Selwyn I'll be along as soon as I can,' he muttered and, giving her a half-grateful grimace, added,
'And. . .er. . .thanks.'

When Paula arrived at the hospital, Selwyn was in a far
worse state than she had imagined. He was a thin, fair

haired man with hard-worked eyes which were hidden behind spectacles. As chartered surveyors, he and Sally had met in the same company where they had worked since their early twenties. They were a close couple and longed for children, and had been on cloud nine, Paula realized, when the immunotherapy had worked so efficiently for them.

Now, though, Selwyn was distraught. 'The heart attack was bad enough,' he told Paula bitterly as she tried to make him sit down in the waiting area closest to Theatre. 'At her age it seems so unfair. I mean, who has a heart attack at thirty-six, for heaven's sake?'

'Possibly more people than you would think,' Paula told him gently. 'But it was a double blow for Sally, being pregnant. Have you heard anything?'

'Only that they're doing a Caesarean.' He shook his head miserably. 'She was fine last night. Oh, hating being in hospital, of course, especially since she's been stuck in the cardiac unit. Everything seemed fine last night, though.'

'Then it was this morning the baby became distressed?'

'They rang me at work and I came straight here. Then I phoned the surgery and they put me through to you as you were free. I couldn't think what else to do. I feel so useless.'

'Sally will need all the support you can give her, Selwyn—just your being there will be of enormous help,' she told him encouragingly.

He looked up. 'I'll give her all the support in the world if only she's all right. If it has to be a choice— if I'm given one—I want Sally, Dr Harvie. I love her so desperately. I don't think I could contemplate life without her.'

Plainly, he was tormenting himself, but the possibilities were always there. One could not ignore them, but

Paula hoped desperately he would never have to be faced with such a choice.

'Hang on in there,' she said kindly. 'The waiting is dreadful, I know, but I'm sure they'll let us know very soon.'

They did.

A few minutes later, the doctor came to speak to them. 'Mr Walker, I'm sorry to have to give you this news. . .' he began dully, and Paula reached out to support Selwyn's arm.

CHAPTER EIGHT

THE death of the Walkers' tiny baby affected Paula deeply.

Louise Sally weighed less than one pound three ounces, and she was so small that when Selwyn was able to hold her he could have slipped his wedding ring over her arm.

He broke down in tears after that and wept. Paula sat with him, feeling numbed. The disbelief that she'd felt with Emily came back in full force; the growing realization of the abrupt ending to new life was so overwhelming that tears came to her eyes and she had to exert all her will-power in order to comfort Selwyn. Through his sobs, she understood, the doctors had told him the baby had not been able to withstand the trauma of the heart attack.

'I just don't know how to console Sally,' he wept. 'All I do know is, I'm so thankful she's all right. But it's not the same for her. She so desperately wanted this baby. There's not a chance of another now.'

Paula knew that Sally must be heartbroken. All she could offer to do was visit later, and Selwyn accepted readily. Leaving him to talk with the hospital social worker who would help him arrange a burial, Paula went to her car. Very carefully she tried to compose herself, but, sinking her face in her hands, she let the heavy, burdensome tears fall, knowing that with them came all her own grief, mixed with the grief for Sally and the baby and the heartrending ache that would take so many years to ease in the Walkers' broken lives.

*　　*　　*

Somehow, later, she managed to ring Sam. She sensed his sadness and bitter disappointment over the phone, but also his resignation. She felt then that he, too, had worried about this pregnancy more than he'd admitted.

When she returned for her three-thirty appointment, he had gone and had left word he would catch up with her later. She managed her short surgery, though by the time she left she felt exhausted from trying to keep her mind objective.

At seven o'clock she was back at the hospital and walking towards the side ward with Selwyn. He seemed resigned now, but Sally was devastated. Paula said nothing, not until Sally was able to find her own words.

Through puffy eyes and quivering lips, Sally poured out her feelings of guilt and loss. She was obsessed with the thought that by taking the pill for so many years and concentrating on her career she had risked what had happened to Louise. The heart attack had convinced her that somehow she was responsible for her baby's death.

'You'll blame yourself over everything for a while,' Paula told her gently, remembering that after Emily's death she had gone over the pregnancy a million times in her mind. 'It's a very natural part of the healing process.'

Sally determinedly shook her head. 'I've read those kind of things in books. You doctors are very kind, but you don't know what it really feels like to lose a baby.'

Paula lifted her chin and hoped her shaky voice would not betray her. 'As it happens, I do, Sally,' she said quietly. 'I lost my little girl Emily in the seventh month of pregnancy. I don't know why—I still think about the reasons which were given to me clinically. All I can say is, it was nature's way of taking her for the best—that I didn't have to watch her suffer or struggle for life.' She blinked her eyes which were moist. 'Being philosophical about her still doesn't take away the pain. I do know what you're going through.'

Sally choked back the tears. 'I. . .I'm sorry, Dr Harvie, I didn't know.'

Paula gave a small shrug. 'My husband was a doctor, too, but we divorced after her death. We didn't have. . .' she glanced at Selwyn, trying to find the right words '. . .the strength that you two have. If we had, we could have helped each other. As you and Selwyn will.'

It was, Paula realized, a major revelation to make to two people whom she had known for less than three months. She was close to tears, but bravely she kept them back. If sharing some of her own loss, at risk the private person she had always locked away then so be it. Perhaps it was time, as she herself recommended to Sally, to heal fully by sharing.

'I'm so sorry if I've intruded on your memories of Emily, Dr Harvie,' Sally sobbed.

Paula squeezed the small fingers. 'I wish I could help. All I can advise is to talk about it to anyone who cares and understands.'

Sally nodded. 'The social worker said the same.'

Paula nodded, holding herself together, but as a tiny sob rose in her own throat she explained she must go.

'Thank you, Dr Harvie,' Selwyn said once they were alone in the corridor. 'You've helped us a lot.'

As Paula left him, she surreptitiously wiped her damp eyes. At least they had not seen just how much she ached with despair for them.

Her thoughts returned inevitably to the past. If only she and Jay could have made a go of it after Emily! His affair had been a mistake, he'd protested, but she'd known in her heart by then that there would be others. Jay was attractive to women—he needed continual reassurance and attention,—as his next wife had discovered to her cost when she, too, had caught him cheating.

When she finally got home that night, she didn't

bother to cook. Thankfully Aunt Steph was at her bridge club, so she sat down by the French windows in the cool breeze. Slowly the tears came. And this time she gave them free passage to flow.

During the following fortnight, Paula made several visits to Sue and baby Jeremy who was putting on weight and feeding like a gannet.

They discussed Sally and decided to visit her together. But, when they arrived at the cardiac unit, they discovered Sally had just been discharged.

'I hesitated over going before,' Sue revealed worriedly to Paula when they returned to the day room. 'It seemed so unfair that I should have such a beautiful, healthy boy. I thought I might be a cruel reminder.'

'Perhaps a visit when she's settled at home?' Paula suggested. 'And perhaps by then Selwyn and Sally will have considered other options for a family.'

'You mean adoption?' Sue said thoughtfully.

'Why not? They've a lovely home and lots of love to give. I'm sure they would make perfect adoptive parents.'

Paula hoped Sue wouldn't fret over Sally. She had had her fair share of trauma with Poppy and Jeremy, and would be one of the few who would genuinely understand Sally's loss. But it was early days yet. Sue had to recuperate herself.

'How are you feeling?' she asked, concerned at Sue's rather pale features.

'Oh, fine,' Sue said over-brightly. Then she sighed, shaking her head. 'Actually I'm not. I'm desperate to go home, but they want Jeremy up a bit in weight before we leave. Is Mrs McDuff coping?'

'Perfectly,' Paula reassured her. 'Mrs McDuff's a born leader.'

'I know she keeps Ken in his place. But Poppy's a handful.'

'Poppy's at the CDC for most of the day, and when she comes home Mrs McDuff can't wait to spoil her whilst you're out of the way.'

The Centre for Disabled Children coped with Poppy adequately in the holidays, but Paula omitted to say that Mrs McDuff had observed once or twice she didn't know how Sue was going to manage with a new baby, Poppy and the practice.

But, when Sue did finally arrive home, the weather was blazing its way into a ferociously hot July. It was a shimmering, golden, heat-hazed Monday morning when Paula fought her way through market day traffic and arrived at work to find Sam walking Mabel on a lead, allowing the puppy to nuzzle the flowers that toppled over the border of the car park.

'Hello, Trouble.' Paula bent to hold the proffered paw.

'How come Mabel gets all the attention these days?' His gaze went admiringly over the soft blue cotton shift she wore. Her legs and arms were lightly tanned with the glorious sunshine and her grey eyes sparkled as she brushed back her freshly washed hair from Mabel's frisky attention.

'She's a sweetie, that's why,' Paula laughed, and her eyes sparkled teasingly.

'And I'm not?'

'If you're fishing for compliments, you're out of luck. I've no idea how sweet you are.'

'Aren't you tempted to find out?' he teased her.

Paula blushed. Her memory still served her well enough to remind her there had been little doubt about the quality of Sam's sweetness!

'Well, obviously not,' he sighed, giving her a shrug which aimed to be casual, but which she knew hid his disappointment. 'Ken's taken Poppy into the centre,' he told her, efficiently instructing Mabel to sit, which she did surprisingly promptly. 'Then he's collecting Sue and Jeremy and bringing them home. We're one less in surgery, one extra on board in the form of Trouble, here, whom Mrs McDuff has flatly refused to have drooling over a brand-new baby. And, I hate to add, Valerie Curry has just walked in and she's booked with you.'

Paula groaned softly. 'What are you going to do with Mabel?'

'Haven't an earthly. What are you going to do with Valerie Curry?'

'Hope,' sighed Paula, 'that I can come up with something pretty quick as she launches her first attack.'

Just then a tall man approached them with a dog that could have been Mabel's double. 'Dr Carlile—Dr Harvie!'

Paula stared in surprise at the transformed figure who was at least half as thin as when she had last seen him. 'Mr Bamford—I am impressed!' she gasped.

'Me, too,' agreed Sam as he struggled to unwrap Mabel's lead from his long legs and the two dogs entered a free-for-all.

'Sorry about this,' Harry Bamford apologized. 'Milo, sit!' Harry laughed, managing to drag an envelope out of his pocket. 'It's an invitation,' he said proudly. 'Janine, my fiancée, and I are getting married in October.'

'Married?' Paula was astonished as Sam wrung their patient's hand vigorously, congratulating him.

'We met just after I had Milo, thanks to you, Dr Carlile. And, thanks to you, Dr Harvie, I decided to persevere with the weight reduction class where I met Janine. We're marrying at St Benedict's.'

Paula threw Sam a wry glance. They had both been wrong and right about Harry Bamford's weight problems. Sam grinned at her.

Harry bent down and fondly stroked Mabel's head. 'She looks great,' he enthused. 'A bit smaller than Milo. Good strong bones, these Labs. Fantastic eyes, don't you think?'

Sam laughed. 'You're obviously hooked.'

Harry nodded as he stood up. 'As a matter of fact, I was just coming in to let you know I've moved. Janine and I have bought a shop in Warwick. A pet shop. We're going to run it between us.'

Paula wished she could have stayed to talk; Harry was a success story if ever there was one, even if the credits were shared! But other matters pressed. She had Valerie Curry to face.

Not only Valerie Curry, she discovered, but Steven Crane who was booked in as her first patient and had managed to acquire himself another spectacular accident trophy in the form of a large gash on his forearm.

'Went swimming last night in Stanpit Lake,' he told her. 'Nothing much else to do. I grazed it on something in the reeds. The last tetanus I had was when I was a kid.'

'Then we'd better give you a shot if you haven't had one recently,' Paula agreed as she cleaned the wound and removed with forceps two tiny shards of reed.

'Ouch!'

'Sorry. They were just beginning to fester.'

'Oh, I don't mind the pain,' Steven said as he watched her clean the wound. 'Things like this fascinate me.'

Paula administered the injection and, after numbing his arm, she gently made five small, neat sutures.

'No job in the offing yet?' Paula asked.

'Not really.' Steven sighed. 'That's why I get so bored. There aren't many job opportunities for someone like me, you know.'

Paula had to smile. Suddenly an idea came to her. 'Have you tried the hospital? Portering, for instance.'

He looked at her blankly. 'Portering?' he repeated.

'Well, you're a fit young man. And your interest obviously lies in medicine. I would have thought the hospital environment would interest you. You've obviously got a strong stomach,' she added dryly.

He gave it some thought as he rolled down his sleeve. 'I'd never get into a place like that. I haven't got references.'

Paula glanced at him under her lids. 'You've got us.'

His face was astonished. 'You mean you'd give me a reference?'

'If you truly wanted the job and felt you could stick to it.'

'I like anywhere medical,' the young man said thoughtfully. 'I often thought I should have been a doctor.'

'Well, you'll need those out in five days.' Paula nodded to his arm and turned away to dispose of her gloves, hiding her smile. 'Make an appointment with the nurse, if you like,' she told him. As her satisfied patient left he informed her he would go into Warwick that day. This time, he didn't ask her for the fare!

Valerie Curry made her entrance soon afterwards. 'Heart,' she puffed. 'Chest pain.'

'Sit down,' Paula said. 'Now, where exactly is the pain?'

Valerie Curry's grandmother, it turned out, had been beset with angina but this revelation had not been discovered in the family archives until the weekend when Valerie had turned out her attic and come across old letters.

Once again Paula thoroughly examined her worried patient. She found no evidence of angina, but she did find something else.

'Did you know you are asthmatic, Mrs Curry?'

The woman looked horrified. 'I certainly am not!'

'The symptoms you've presented me with are consistent with asthma, not angina. Breathlessness accompanied by a painless tightness in the chest. Wheezing—which my stethoscope has picked up this morning—I suspect brought on by the dust mites in your attic, since you also complained of an unusual bout of runny nose and feeling unwell.' Paula walked behind her patient, pulled back her shoulders from their stooped position so she was sitting straight and manoeuvred her arms to support her chest. 'Does that feel better?'

Valerie Curry was clearly shocked, however she did manage to nod.

'It helps sometimes to sit more comfortably.' Paula returned to her desk and keyboarded in a prescription. 'I'm going to give you an aerosol inhalant to relieve your symptoms. It's easy enough to take. But you'd be far better off avoiding dust and watching out for anything which seems to precipitate an attack. How are the haemorrhoids?' Paula asked as a parting shot.

It was the quietest Valerie Curry had ever been. 'Oh. . .fine,' she dismissed vaguely. 'Asthma! Whoever would have believed I have asthma?'

After Valerie, Paula rocketed through her morning. At lunch time John asked her if she'd like a bite to eat at the Beeswax, and they demolished two rounds of prawn sandwiches smothered in dressing. John told her that Sue had arrived home, and before Paula made her afternoon calls she popped in to the house and found Sam in the hall, holding the baby.

'He seems to have the knack,' Sue said, lifting rueful eyebrows. 'He's been yelling continually since I brought him home but shut up like a clam when Sam started rocking him.'

'It's the technique,' Sam boasted.

Sue and Paula grinned as Jeremy let out an ear-shattering wail.

'Back to Mum,' Sam muttered, gently passing the

white bundle. 'I can tell you one thing,' he said as Sue rocked him in her arms, 'that's a hungry cry. He's ravenous.'

Sue lifted her eyes. 'Another feed, you little monster?'

'Bath's ready,' Ken said, rushing in from the bathroom with a pinny tied around his waist. I've time enough to scrub him down before surgery,' he said, wielding a massive orange bath brush.

Everyone burst into laughter.

'You idiot,' laughed Sue.

Ken fondly slipped an arm around her waist. 'What do you think of my son and heir?' he chuckled proudly.

'Nothing like you at all,' said Sam rudely. 'He's Sue's features and eyes and small ears—maybe he has your feet. Now smile, because I'm going to take pictures for posterity.' He whipped up his camcorder from a chair and before anyone could move he had captured Jeremy's homecoming.

Ken groaned afterwards. 'I just hope something of the Dunwoody thoroughbred comes through on film!'

Paula giggled. 'Don't worry, Ken, they say the trade marks develop with age.'

'Lord help him,' Sue gasped, patting her husband's generous girth. 'I'm sure Ken's been having a phantom pregnancy with me. Trouble is, his phantom doesn't know when it's over.'

In the midst of their laughter, Mrs McDuff called from the study. 'The CDC can't drop Poppy back this afternoon. The minibus has broken down. Can someone collect her, please?'

'I'll go!' volunteered Sam loudly, shuffling the camcorder into its case. 'Time and place, please, Mrs McDuff!'

Sue looked up in surprise. 'Are you sure, Sam?'

'Four-thirty, is it? Or thereabouts? I'm finished at four. And I have to go to Warwick to collect Mabel.'

'Mabel?' everyone chorused.

Sam grinned. 'Harry Bamford's installed her in his pet shop with his Lab for the day. Apparently they've kennels and a garden—Mabel accepted the offer like a shot.'

'That's our rather large man with ankylosing spondylitis, isn't it?' Ken queried.

'Was our large man,' corrected Paula. 'He's lost weight, found himself a fiancée and a new career.'

'And he's off the anti-inflammatories,' Sam provided. 'He's still in physio, but he's down to twice a month now.'

'Amazing what love can do,' murmured Sue, glancing ruefully at her husband.

'Amazing,' agreed Sam, amusement in his eyes as he glanced under his heavy lids at Paula.

The pattern of ills remained unchanged from previous years Paula discovered, as during the hottest month of the year sun-stroke and exhaustion became the besetting complains of visitors and locals alike.

Paula visited Mrs Lessing one scalding day and was glad of the opportunity because she had been meaning to see how she was coping after her husband's death earlier in the summer.

A neighbour had called, saying that Mrs Lessing hadn't been seen for a couple of days. When she'd let herself in the house, the old lady had been unable to get up from the settee.

The same neighbour, a Mrs Shapley, let Paula in. 'She's not good,' she told Paula worriedly. 'Not at all.'

Mrs Lessing, Paula discovered, was extremely ill. She was delirious, pale, clammy and her pulse was faint. She didn't look as if she'd eaten or washed in days, and Paula guessed her weight had dropped dramatically from the last time she'd seen her.

'I'm going to ring for an ambulance,' Paula told the neighbour. 'Could you put a few things together for her? A nightie and slippers and so on?'

Mrs Shapley hurried off, saying she'd have everything ready in a jiffy. Paula rang the hospital and then went back to her patient. As she was listening to the worryingly faint heartbeat, Mrs Lessing opened her eyes and seemed suddenly aware of her surroundings.

'Who's that?' she said softly. Her eyes seemed to look beyond Paula into the distance, but she smiled and grasped Paula's hand.

'I'm Dr Harvie,' said Paula gently. 'I don't know if you remember me, but I saw you some months ago. How are you feeling, Mrs Lessing?'

The old lady sighed. 'I thought you were a dream. I thought you were my Albert.'

Paula leaned over her. 'Mrs Lessing. . .?'

But her eyes had closed again, and Paula felt her pulse. Every now and then it became faint, only to struggle up briefly to pace again. Paula went to the kitchen to pour a glass of water for the parched lips. The rancid odour almost overpowered her. She opened the fridge and found the cause of the problem. Tray upon tray from meals on wheels, all stacked upon one another—untouched.

Soon the ambulance came and Mrs Lessing was taken on board.

'Are there no relatives?' Paula asked the neighbour.

'None that I know of. Only the meals lady calls and me. I've got a key and I check every couple of days. But lately Dorothy wouldn't ask me in. I think she's ready to go,' Mrs Shapley observed bluntly. 'She kept saying Albert was waiting. I really think she believes it. She says she talks to him all the time.'

Paula nodded. 'She thought I was him.'

'There were very close,' Mrs Shapley said philosophically. 'Too close to enjoy life without one another.'

Paula frowned. 'She must have been very lonely.'

'They were like peas in a pod. Your doctor Carlile will tell you. He knew Albert. Came to see him pretty often, he did.'

'Was he unwell?'

'Only with a bit of angina. Dr Carlile tried to persuade him to give up smoking and take long walks, but he was a home-bird. And that old pipe of his was on the go constantly. Oh well, I'll go to the hospital this evening and take her some grapes.'

Paula thanked her. Then she wrapped the detritus in the fridge in newspapers and plastic bags and finally dustbin liners and put it with the refuse. She locked the back door and closed the front one firmly behind her. By the time she had finished her evening surgery, the sad news came from the hospital that Mrs Lessing had passed away.

To Paula's further surprise, when she told Sam she was going to attend the funeral he said he had already arranged flowers to be sent from the surgery.

'Mrs Lessing's neighbour explained you knew Albert,' she said. It was a muggy, overcast August morning and the service was arranged for ten at Struan's St Benedict's.

'Albert was keen on cameras, too,' he explained simply. 'I would have come with you,' he added as he nodded to one of his patients in the full waiting room. 'But as you can see I've a long list.' His face softened as he brought back his gaze to her face, his tone gentle as he went on. 'But perhaps when you visit Emily next. . .' he hesitated, searching her eyes. 'If you wouldn't object to some company, then?'

She was shocked as she wondered if he really meant it. 'Emily's memorial is in London, close to where we

lived,' she murmured in surprise, but when she saw the
sincerity in his gaze she swallowed, nodding. 'But. . .
thank you. Yes, perhaps when I go next. . .'

He gave her arm a gentle squeeze. 'Good. Don't forget.' Then, bringing back his broad shoulders and
smiling, he frowned ruefully, quirking one dark eyebrow. 'As a matter of fact, I was going to ask you if
you had a few hours spare this weekend. I'm taking
Poppy out for a few hours to give Ken and Sue a bit of
free time with the baby. Come with us.'

Paula hesitated, biting her lip and sighing. 'This
weekend. . .' she mumbled doubtfully.

'Poppy will be hopelessly disappointed. I've already
told her, you see.' He grinned, shrugging innocently.

Paula gave him a wry grimace. 'Why is it I can never
say no when Poppy's involved?'

'Beats me. I'll just have to go on hoping that one day
you'll say yes for my company alone. I'll call for you
at ten. Better go now.' Casting her a wicked grin, he
disappeared into his room.

She stared after him, amazed she could suddenly feel
so transformed when she thought of being with him
again—the tingling spine, the rapidly accelerating pulse,
an unreasonable anticipation. . .

'Hadn't you better shoot off, Dr Harvie?' Bella called
as she swept down the hallway 'It's five to.'

Paula started. 'Oh. . .oh, yes, thanks, Bella.'

With a firm effort she drew herself up and put herself
into gear. Her heart was still racing at the thought of
being with Sam again—and yet what could it lead to?
A brief affair before he left for the other side of he
world and she hurtled back to London? Was that what
she really wanted? A distracting anaesthetic for a few
months?

She tried to put the thought of it from her mind as
she attended Mrs Lessing's short service in the little

chapel of Saint Benedict. Mrs Shapley was there, and a small group of neighbours. Together with the vicar they bade farewell. Sam's beautiful bouquet of pink and white carnations spilled generously over the polished wood of the coffin, and the organ managed a rattley version of the Twenty-Third Psalm.

'Life's pretty precious,' sighed Mrs Shapley beside her. 'Might as well enjoy every moment of it whilst you're here. I've known Albert and Dorothy for forty-five years and it seems like the blink of an eye. Just to think I'll never be going in that house again to see how she is.'

Paula found herself nodding. Suddenly she wanted, more than anything, to be with Sam.

She could have driven them in the Polo, she realized.

Instead, Sam insisted on calling for her in the Mercedes and then driving back to collect Poppy. The reason, she suspected, was that his passenger would be dependent on him for the day, and she felt a warm sense of belonging fill her as she thought of it.

He arrived promptly, dressed in jeans and a dark blue T-shirt. He seemed to have become even more tanned over the last few weeks. His rich jet-black hair and dark eyes shone out like pools of ink as he chatted with Aunt Steph in the garden whilst Paula collected her sports bag from the house. She wore new jeans and a pretty blue and white polka dot blouse in a soft silky material.

'Ready,' she said at last, discovering Sam deep in conversation with Aunt Steph. He looked up and his eyes flew over her admiringly.

'I'm sorry to have spoiled your Saturday,' he said unrepentantly to her aunt. 'Dragging Paula off like this.'

Aunt Steph shook her head. 'Oh, not at all! I like to see Paula enjoying herself. To my mind, she doesn't socialize enough.'

Sam threw Paula a curious glance and she blushed. 'See you later, Aunt Steph,' she interrupted before any more skeletons fell out of the closet.

Enjoy yourselves,' Aunt Steph called breezily, waving goodbye.

Sam leaned across to help her with the seat belt as they sat in the car. Somehow his mouth managed to brush against her ear. 'Now,' he whispered threateningly, sending a frisson of electricity down her spine, 'I've got you all to myself. What am I going to do with you?' Then his lips covered hers and, despite the fear of Aunt Steph seeing, Paula slid her arms around his neck and closed her eyes as he explored the surprising welcome of her open mouth.

'That was. . .' he said huskily as he leaned back, frowning at her, 'Very, *very* different.'

She laughed nervously. 'Was it?'

He nodded, leaning over to her once more. 'I'm going to threaten you more often. It appears to work wonders.'

She waited for her ragged breathing to return to normal before she allowed herself to stare into his dark brown irises. 'I'm glad I came,' she whispered, 'very glad.'

He stared back at her, his eyes running over her, as though trying to figure out what had changed. She had scooped her hair into a pleat to keep it out of the way and silky blonde tendrils escaped from the pins to curl around her ears. She wore only a little lipstick, and as he clasped a hand softly around her neck to draw her closer she was sure the remnant she had left on her trembling lips would soon be gone.

'Poppy?' she reminded him softly, and he grinned, sliding a predatory tongue over his top lip before he finally let her go and reached out to switch on the engine. She sat back, deliriously happy, and drank in the heavenly morning. He drove steadily, eventually extri-

cating them from a busy Marble Lane and past the castle
to the Struan road.

'Did I tell you Sue's taking an emergency surgery
this morning—her first since the baby?' he asked as
he drove.

Paula was surprised. 'How will she manage with
Jeremy?'

'Ken's doing the honours. But I suspect Mrs McDuff
will be hovering in the background just to see everything
runs smoothly.'

Paula thought how swiftly Sue had managed to adapt.
She was full of admiration for her—only two months
post birth. And yet, of course, with Jeremy being both
early and having a healthy recovery, wasn't it a sign
that the practice itself would be returning to a normal
routine?

She could quite envisage them not wanting her by
Christmas. In all fairness, she must speak to Sue about
it. The last thing she wanted was for Sue to feel obliged
to keep her after December if there was no necessity.

'I had some news this week,' Sam said suddenly as
he put the car into top gear on the open road. 'Jilly's
finally turned up. She's signed the Lorimar agreement.'

Not one bombshell, but two, Paula thought, catching
her breath and trying to look reasonably composed.
'Congratulations, Sam,' she said quietly. 'I really am
pleased for you.'

'It means the unit is up and running—and there's
enough money for specialist treatment and new equip-
ment for the next decade.'

And had Jilly Cameron delivered the news personally? Paula wondered bleakly. She remembered the face
on the video. The beautiful copper hair and the tawny
skin. Jilly Cameron had reached almost mythic pro-
portions in her mind, and she blinked trying to rid herself
of the painful pang of jealousy.

'Idiot!' Sam suddenly muttered as a car streaked between them and the car in front, forcing him to hit the brake pedal and swerve out of harm's way.

Paula clung to the seat as the skid brought her with a bump back to reality. The driver of the speeding car seemed to increase his speed, and pulled out into the middle of the road. Then with a horrendous squeal of tyres he braked, slowed down so that he was equal with them and then in one violent jerk crashed in on their bumper, sending a sickening shudder through the Mercedes.

'Madman!' cursed Sam, but the next thing she knew he was having to fight with the wheel as the car in front once more lurched across their path. To avoid the reckless driving of the lunatic Sam was forced to pull over onto the hard shoulder just as the car bonnet seemed to lift in front of them, glide smoothly into the air, dip again and bounce frantically down a slope.

She remembered hearing the eerie slap of tiny, help-less saplings as their branches broke over the windscreen, feeling her throat constrict as Sam's arm came across her in a swift, reflexive, protective move-ment as the car went out of control.

CHAPTER NINE

POSSIBLY the fact that Sam had ensured her safety with his swift action had also rendered him more likely to be injured. . .

At least, this was what the SHO tried to explain as he and Sam argued over the fractured ulna bone in his left arm. Lying in a hospital bed in the medical ward with a chunk out of his forehead and absolutely no clear memory of the last hour did nothing to diminish Sam's sense of injustice that he was being made to remain in hospital unnecessarily.

Paula sat in the chair beside the bed, miraculously unscathed, shaken and shaking still, but she was amazed that Sam had still remained conscious after the blow he'd taken on the head as they had hurtled to the bottom of the ditch.

At that point she hadn't realized he'd also hurt his arm as he'd struggled to release her from her seat belt to haul her out of the hissing, steaming car. It wasn't until the ambulance had arrived ten minutes later and the paramedics had persuaded Sam—who had been sitting on the bank with her as she'd tried to mop up the open wound on his forehead as best she could—to let them treat him that he'd let out a fairly substantial groan.

'This is absurd,' Sam was complaining as the SHO flatly refused to waver. 'Look, I can walk a straight line, I can remember my birthday and who is Prime Minister. A skid in a car isn't going to put me out of action for the whole weekend, not if I have anything to do with it—'

'Which you haven't,' said the young doctor. 'You're

plastered up to the elbow. You've concussion and I want you to have a scan.'

'But I got out of the car—'

'Lord knows how, but yes.'

'I got out of the car,' Sam continued, grimacing. 'I had a touch of mild concussion, perhaps—'

'Would you allow a patient home in your condition?' the SHO posed sharply. 'I hardly think you'd waste time arguing with them.'

'I'm trying to save you a bed,' Sam muttered, unwilling to give up the fight.

'I think we can manage to budget you this one.' The doctor beckoned the ward sister, took her aside and began to give her firm instructions about Sam, closing the curtains behind him so Sam could not interrupt.

'How come they're not keeping *you* in for obs?' he demanded crossly.

'Perhaps because I haven't an egg on my head the size of Everest,' answered Paula wryly. 'And, apart from a little shock, I think I can handle getting up and walking out of here, which I seriously doubt you could do at this moment.'

'Try me. I've a hairline fracture, that's all.'

'And, apart from being horrendously painful, it'll take several weeks to knit.'

'I refuse to lug this thing for the next two weeks—'

'I'm afraid you haven't any choice.' Paula sighed. 'Look, the more you protest the more they're likely to keep you on your backside thinking you really have lost your little grey cells.'

This, she was pleased to see, shut him up. He sat there glowering, his right hand going up to touch the gauze patch on his forehead under which eight firm sutures had been effectively planted.

'We're taking you down for a scan, Dr Carlile,' Sister

said as she drew back the curtain. 'May I suggest Dr Harvie gets a little rest herself?'

Sam glanced at Paula. 'How are you going to get home?'

She shrugged. 'Aunt Steph's is five minutes by taxi. Ken offered to come when I phoned him, but I asked him instead to sort out the recovery of the Mercedes after the police have done with it.'

Sister looked at Sam levelly. 'There, you see? The world can obviously get along without you quite nicely for a bit. And perhaps you'll be happy to know that the police have arrested the driver of the car who forced you off the road. He was way over the limit—hadn't a clue what he was doing.'

Sam frowned. 'Pleasant character.'

'I think I had better go.' Paula stood up slowly. She was determined not to let Sam see how shaky she still felt, but he lifted a knowing eyebrow which she realized must have been quite painful under the gauze. As Sister tactfully left them alone, he reached out for her hand and pulled her towards him. 'Are you really in a fit state to find a taxi?'

'I'm fine,' she reassured him. 'Not a scratch in sight.'

He let out something that sounded like a growl. 'What a mess to get you into.'

She sunk to the bed and wrapped her fingers around his hand. 'Sam, you were the one who took the brunt of the crash. Thanks to you, I'm sitting here in one piece.'

He looked up at her with huge dark eyes as she bent to brush her lips on his cheek, but his good hand snaked out around her head, bringing her lips to his mouth. 'I can still kiss,' he threatened, showing her exactly what he meant. His mouth was warm and sweet, and she closed her eyes, forgetting all else as she kissed him longingly back, aware that nothing in the world mattered more now than this.

Fortunately, Mrs McDuff had coped with Poppy after Paula had phoned from the hospital. Sue had ploughed on with her surgery and Ken had organized the Mercedes. That left Trouble.

Remembering Sam left a spare key to the cottage in his desk at work, Paula dug it out, drove over to the surgery and went through a brief summary of what had happened for Ken and Sue's benefit.

Mabel was in the process of causing mayhem with Poppy, and Jeremy was bringing the house down. Paula tactfully swept Mabel into the Polo and drove back, albeit it still shakily to the cottage—she wasn't sure if it was the reaction from Sam's kiss or the accident. Mabel christened the lawn immediately and promptly barked to be let in.

'You're not hungry yet.' Paula walked carefully into the kitchen.

The puppy disagreed and barked at the fridge.

Well, perhaps you are,' she relented and went to dig out a meal from the canister which Sam kept for her. It was, of course, empty. So was the cupboard *and* the freezer.

With a sigh, Paula sat down in the front room and Mabel clambered onto her lap. Before long, she found herself drawn into sleep, and along with Mabel's deep, steady breathing she drifted off.

Mabel awoke her at four-thirty, when Mrs Next Door began mowing the lawn. Groggily Paula phoned her aunt to say she would not be back for supper as planned, then she made a brief shopping list, drove to the local store in Struan and returned to feed Mabel and fill the cupboards with goodies.

Feeling better for the sleep, she took a shower,

changed into the trousers and T-shirt she kept as a spare in the car and made herself a quick meal of scrambled eggs. After walking Mabel in the nearby wood, she settled her back into the cottage and geared herself towards a drive to the hospital.

'Visiting's almost over,' Sam informed her miserably as she arrived.

'Did you have your scan?' She tugged the curtains around the bed in order to help him change his clothing.

'Waste of time. I could have told them both pieces of brain were still intact.'

She heaved the hold-all onto the bed. 'Robe, slippers, toothbrush and flannel, razor and fresh pyjamas—'

'I don't wear pyjamas,' he told her challengingly, his dark eyes glinting.

She'd had a quick rummage through his drawers at the cottage and come to the same conclusion herself. 'These are new ones.' She tried to ignore the enticing look on his face as she shook out the jacket.

'I'll only be able to wear the bottoms.' He gave her a mischievous smile. 'You can have the top—providing you model it for me.' Before she could protest, he was hauling her against his hard body, his mouth coming down to claim hers as she fell across the bed and, after a second or two, she gave into his pressure, feeling the beat of his heart through the soft linen, gently wrapping her arms around all the undamaged pieces of torso.

'We shouldn't be doing this,' she whispered, as a shudder of tingling desire travelled through her, his kiss gentling as she looked into his face. 'It's breaking all the rules—'

'All the more reason,' he pleaded, 'for them to chuck me out. Then you could nurse me at home.' His face was suddenly serious, the teasing grin gone and only the depths of seriousness left in his expression. 'Would you, Paula? Would you come home with me?'

She stared into the craggy, bruised face, wanting to tell him she would like nothing more, ever, than to lie with him like this, to be wrapped in his strong arms, to feel his solidity beneath her fingers—to know that every day would be the same, to be assured of his presence in her life. And she also knew that in a clumsy, foggy way he was asking her if she wanted to be part of his life. 'I'd come,' she whispered tremblingly, 'if you wanted me. . .'

A shudder ran through her, as, without speaking, he bent again to kiss her with a kiss that seemed to seal their mutual understanding. All she wanted now was a chance to prove her love for him, to let him be aware of how much she wanted him in her life. Crazy, in a hospital ward, to decide the future! she thought as she kissed him back, gently stroking her fingers over his stubbled jaw, feeling the tiny pinpricks of beard nuzzle electrically under her skin, tantalizing and teasing her until she almost forgot where she was.

'Oh, Paula,' he groaned sweetly against her lips. 'Paula. . .' He ran his fingers through her hair, making her shudder with sensation as the touch across her neck sent waves of pleasure through her body, and she gulped, trying to sit up a little, suddenly aware that a head might come around the curtain.

'You look beautiful tonight. And I can't do a damned thing about it,' he groaned, refusing to let her sit up. 'This is torture—'

'Sam. . .we'll have to be patient,' she mumbled, her body throbbing with intensity. The pyjamas, totally forgotten, lay strewn across the bed. He kissed her again, and then, sighing deeply, he reluctantly let her go as she stood to her feet, smoothing down her blouse and skirt.

She ached to reach down and thread her fingers through his hair, gently soothe his battered head.

He sighed, leaning back his head. 'When the car left

the road this morning, I thought of all the things that were important to me in this world. There was only one person I was concerned about. . .one person who meant everything to me. . .'

There was a lump in her throat as she swallowed. 'Me, too,' she whispered. 'Me, too.'

'Will I see you tomorrow?'

'Ring me. Let me know what time to collect you.'

'The crack of dawn be OK?'

She grinned. 'I'll be waiting.'

He looked at her with desire-filled eyes. 'I want you, Paula, every little piece of you. Body and soul.'

Her heart thudded as she bent to kiss him for the last time. 'Sleep well, my darling.' She dragged away her hand and somehow extricated herself from the strong grip, turning to pull back the curtains.

'Tomorrow,' he whispered as she felt herself blushing at the enquiring gaze of the man in the next bed.

She nodded, mouthing, 'Tomorrow.'

'I want you, Paula. I want to hold you and have you near to me without the whole damn world gazing in.'

She shook her head, moving to the end of the bed. 'Bye, Sam,' she choked and then she flew from the ward, not daring to look back.

She awoke from a deep sleep in Sam's bed—sniffing in the aroma from his pillow, making her remember the way he had smelt and felt as she'd kissed him at the hospital. She'd been dreaming of him, but any hope of remembering it faded when the telephone shrieked at eight. She sat up in bed, rubbing her eyes, reaching out to grapple with the extension.

'It's me,' Sam said in a wounded, muffled voice. 'They won't let me home.'

She blinked, trying to focus. 'Oh, Sam, is everything all right?'

He was trying to cover his emotions, and his voice came gruffly over the line. 'They refuse to let me home today because that young snake went off duty giving instructions he wanted to see me tomorrow morning with the scan results—'

'Which is probably the best thing because of the concussion,' Paula interrupted, thinking she had better try to make the best of the situation.

'Paula, I miss you—'

'It won't be long,' she soothed, sinking back into the bed, feeling miserably disappointed.

'I wish I was there. Did you sleep—?'

'Here in your bed,' she whispered. 'On your pillow.'

'Oh, God. Don't tell me. . .'

'Sam?' She gathered her sleepy senses, holding the phone closely as she whispered softly, 'Do you really mean it? Do you want me here when you come home?'

'I want you there—always. Not just now, tomorrow, whenever, but always. Damn. If only I could see you, hold you. . .'

'Sam—' Suddenly there was an alarm ringing, and the intimate moment dissolved into thin air as she realized it was her bleeper on the table. 'Sam, I'm on call today. Listen. . .I'll try to get in to see you later, but if I don't you'll know why—'

'Bloody bleeper,' she heard before she was forced to put down the phone.

The signal was from Sue who'd had a call from Mrs Matthews. Damien had fallen sick overnight, and she was worried that it might be the same bronchitis that Paula had treated earlier in the summer.

Throwing on white trousers and a casual shirt, Paula pushed a reluctant and sleepy Mabel into the garden, gulping back an instant coffee as she did so.

When she arrived at the Matthews' house, Damien was being sick. She helped Mrs Matthews prize him from the loo, and managed to take his temperature which was fevered. The boy's face was white and his body was clammy.

'Perhaps a light sponge over it, Mrs Matthews,' Paula suggested, 'to make him feel a little fresher.'

'My tummy hurts and I feel sick,' Damien said, curling into a ball on the bed, bringing his knees up to his stomach.

'He's been in the loo all night.' His mum sighed. 'I wouldn't have thought there was much more to bring up.'

Paula felt around his stomach for nasty lumps or anything remotely suspicious, but, finding nothing other than a very aggrieved abdomen from retching, she helped Mrs Matthews wash him down. Just as they'd finished, he was up again and into the bathroom.

'What did he eat yesterday?' Paula asked as she brought out several sachets of Dioralyte from her case.

'Same as us,' Mrs Matthews said. 'And none of us are ill.'

'He didn't eat anything you didn't?'

'Nothing. He was at home all day playing games on his computer. I would've known if he'd eaten something different.'

Paula nodded. 'In that case it's probably a viral infection.'

Damien hobbled back to bed, drenched in sweat once more. His mother towelled him down again and pulled over the sheets.

'Let's try some of this,' Paula suggested, and they made Damien a drink of the Dioralyte. He sipped half of it and kept it down.

'I'll wait a bit longer,' Paula told Mrs Matthews. 'He should be on the mend if he can manage one or two sips more.'

'What will it do?' Mrs Mathews asked.

'It's an electrolyte solution,' Paula explained, 'which will help to stabilize him, put back what he's lost from the sickness.'

'But where did he catch it from?' Mrs Matthews frowned. 'All the rest of the family are well.'

Paula shook her head. 'It's not easy to say. Viruses are too small to be visible, and trying to identify a source is like looking for a needle in a haystack.'

'Wouldn't some of the Amoxil help him? It did with the bronchitis.'

Paula sighed. 'Antibiotics are ineffective against viruses, I'm afraid. Some viral diseases we can control with vaccines, but this is something Damien will overcome himself.'

Damien groaned, turned a pasty grey and brought his knees up to his stomach. Paula left the Dioralyte on the bedside table and ran her hand over his hot forehead.

'You'll soon be feeling better, Damien,' she said, and with half a yawn and half a groan the seven-year-old closed his eyes.

Ten minutes later he was asleep and Paula was on her way, telling Mrs Matthews to ring in if she was still worried. Even before Paula reached the cottage the mobile phone went and Kylie Grant's distressed voice begged Paula to hurry to the flat.

Without returning to the surgery, Paula hurried to Kylie's. Jasmine was yelling her heart out and George was almost as fretful, rubbing his fists across his eyes and joining in with Jasmine every few minutes.

'They had a terrible night,' Kylie croaked. 'And just before I called you Jasmine went rigid and rolled her eyes. . .it was so frightening.'

Paula nodded, reaching out to take Jasmine. She was very hot, but her lungs were healthy enough. Removing both the babies from their romper suits, she examined each of them as Kylie and Mark looked on.

Paula discovered a slightly swollen lump on each baby, barely larger than pinpricks. She looked up and smiled. 'Have they recently had their DTPs?'

Mark nodded. 'Yesterday. Dr Dunwoody did it for us at her morning surgery because we couldn't get along to clinic.'

'Ah,' Paula nodded, relieved. 'Sometimes the diphtheria, tetanus and pertussis can cause a baby to be fretful and feverish—even produce a fever fit, as we call it, like Jasmine had. It's not common—about one child in ten thousand may have a small convulsion. I'll give you some paracetamol syrup which will help her, although frankly I think you've seen the worst.'

Kylie sighed, closing her eyes. 'Thank goodness for that.' She brought her hands over her face, and as she drew them slowly down Paula saw the ring. Kylie blinked as she met Paula's surprised gaze.

'We took the plunge,' Kylie admitted shyly, and stretched out her hand where the slim band of gold glittered on her finger. 'In the registry office on Wednesday—which is why we couldn't manage clinic.'

Paula stepped forward and hugged her young patient. 'Congratulations,' she said delightedly. 'That's wonderful. Are you happy?'

Kylie nodded. 'We both are. I realized Mark really does care for me. I'm willing to take the chance our marriage will work.'

Paula nodded, thinking it had taken courage to do what Kylie had, and yet they seemed to be much happier—despite Jasmine's hiccup, there was an atmosphere of real contentment and Kylie looked as though she was blossoming.

They crept from the twins' room just a few seconds before her bleeper sounded. She would have liked to accept the cup of tea Mark offered but she found herself on the road again, flying to a suspected heart attack on the other side of the village. By the time she arrived, her sixty-eight-year-old male patient had recovered from a severe angina attack brought on from lifting a too heavy wheelbarrow.

After a thorough examination and a check of the medication he was using to manage the angina, Paula found herself back at the cottage supervising Mabel. She made tea and wondered if she should phone Sam. But by six she was on the road again, back to Damien Matthews who was still complaining of stomach pain.

Mrs Matthews informed her he'd managed to keep down the Dioralyte, and he was certainly looking brighter despite his unwillingness to say he felt better. By the time she had satisfied herself that his main complaint—strained tummy muscles—was no more than pain brought on by the retching, it was early evening.

She put all thoughts of Sam from her mind, fell fast asleep on the sofa and was woken at midnight by the telephone. During the next hour she attended a patient whom she'd suspected had biliary colic. By the time she diagnosed possible gallstones and the necessity of an ultrasound to discover the existence of the small, sharp crystalline stones that were giving such discomfort in the gallbladder, it was half past one in the morning.

She finally hauled herself into bed, too tired to dissuade Mabel from occupying the comfortable chair beside it.

On Monday, her half-day, it poured with rain.

She was surprised not to hear from Sam in the morning and wondered why he had not rung. She drove into the surgery, leaving the answer machine on in case he should call. In surgery she computed her weekend visits, arranged for the gallstone patient to be seen by appointment at the hospital and then escaped, driving home through sunshine and showers. The answer machine's red light was undisturbed.

After showering she emerged refreshed, and decided she would go, without phoning, to the hospital. She took care dressing, her heart thrumming as she thought of bringing Sam home and making him a meal.

A picture of domestic harmony filled her mind. She knew she was being foolish, playing games. But she couldn't resist. Sam with his plaster, sprawled in his chair—she in the kitchen, creating a delicious supper. The rain would be falling against the windows. . . summer rain, which was always soft and magical. They would be cosy inside, eating at the little table again. She'd spotted some candles in a drawer. It would be an intimate evening and they would talk until the early hours. . .

She wore a long skirt in swirling colours, a silk blouse to tone with the pale pink orchids in the skirt, navy pumps and a thin velvet band of cerise in her hair. She felt feminine and fresh and excited. She had turned her mind away from everything except enjoying bringing Sam home. What resulted afterwards—she would let happen. . .

Paula hurried through the corridors, up one flight of stairs and approached the men's medical ward. She gazed along the line of beds. Sam wasn't there.

Her heart dropped. She should have phoned this morning. The bed was neatly made, no new occupant as yet. She checked the locker just to be sure and found it empty.

Paula went to Sister's office which was deserted. She looked around, unable to see a face she recognized. Instinct drew her to the phone in the day room. Just as she dialled the surgery's number, where almost certainly Sue or Ken would know what had happened to him, she

saw the back of a familiar figure through the small pane
of glass in the door.

Her throat went dry, her pulse raced. She let the phone
fall back into the holder and walked towards the door.
Through the glass she saw Sam walking through the
exit, his plastered arm carefully hidden by a sweater
thrown over his shoulders.

He was far too absorbed in the beautiful woman walking by his side to notice Paula as Jilly Cameron slipped
with him through the swing doors.

Paula found herself following. She trailed them at a
distance to the main entrance foyer and watched them
walk to the car park. As the sleek white Porsche swept
by she saw Sam's dark features in the passenger side.

Wasn't it only this morning she had been fantasing
about a romantic evening alone with him. In despair,
she took herself back to the Polo and drove home to
Aunt Steph's. She stepped over the puddles which had
been made by the morning's downpour, entered her
porch and burst into tears.

It was some time later when the phone rang. Paula
answered it, fighting to keep the tremor from her voice.
Despite what had happened, her heart leapt when she
heard his voice. 'Paula?' he demanded. 'Where have
you been?'

'At the hospital.' She tried to keep calm. 'Where have
you been?'

'I waited all day,' he complained, not answering her
question. 'What the devil is going on?'

'I was there at four, Sam.'

'Precisely my point,' he grumbled. 'Damn it woman,
where were you this morning?'

'In your cottage,' she defended, her voice rising,
'looking after your dog, waiting for your phone call.
When you didn't call, I went into surgery.'

'I couldn't phone in the morning,' he told her as though he was surprised she didn't know. 'The doctor's rounds were late. Didn't you get my message?'

'I haven't heard from you all day, Sam—and you know it.'

'You're not making sense, Paula,' he told her irritably. 'I left a message on the answer machine—'

'Well, if you did, I never heard it.' Her voice hitched.

'Paula, what's wrong? There's something wrong, isn't there?'

'Nothing at all.' She told herself she wasn't going to burst into tears—she would rather die than let him see how he had wounded her.

'Then why are you there?' he asked her softly. 'And not here. . .in my arms. . .where you should be?'

'For the simple reason,' she said raggedly, 'that you managed to find your way home quite successfully without me.' Choking back a sob, she put a fist to her mouth and stifled her gasp.

Convince me, she prayed, give me some explanation—make everything all right again. Make some excuse, Sam. . .

But he remained silent. The few seconds seemed like hours before she could bear it no longer. 'G. . .goodnight Sam,' she managed, and put the phone down.

She sank onto the sofa and buried her head in her arms. How could she have been such a fool? How could she have talked herself into loving him?

Oh, God, she loved him—which was why her heart was breaking now.

Paula asked Ken to fetch her things from Sam's.

Ken returned with them and without a message. He said very little, looking painfully embarrassed. She'd had the vicarious thrill of Sam's presence when she'd unfolded her belongings and placed them in a drawer, thinking of Sam's fingers threading through them and folding them into the case. She knew how it was to be the recipient of those fingers. . .

As it was, two weeks without him around the place had steeled her to his return. It was a mellow, bonfire-scented September day when Sam walked back into surgery and strode across Reception.

'Hi, Dr Carlile!' the girls called, and Paula, who was on her way to Sue's room, nodded, stepping aside to let him pass.

But he stopped and stared down at her, completely disarming her with his dark stare. 'Hello, Paula.'

'Sam.' She was sure her voice trembled as she spoke, but no one seemed to notice.

She brought herself sharply back to reality as she moved away swiftly and went to finish her discussion with Sue. She found it almost impossible to concentrate. Leadenly she walked to the window in Sue's room and stared out at the thick copse of autumn-coloured trees. Sue was now able to leave Jeremy with Mrs McDuff whilst Poppy was at school. Paula had all but tied up her leaving date, for November.

'I don't want you to go,' Sue told her regretfully as she joined Paula at the window. 'Won't you consider staying on with us? With you and Sam gone, it won't be the same at Struan House.'

Paula arrested the sensation of falling—the sensation she felt whenever she thought of Sam returning to Delhi.

'We need another female doctor,' Sue persisted generously. 'Our patient list has increased whilst you've been here. You've a surgery of your own—patients who will be disappointed if you leave—especially the antenatal clinic. Just think of all the babies you'll never see born— all those mums whom you'll miss delivering.'

Paula smiled. 'Thank you, Sue—but I've made up my mind.'

'Who's going to miss who?' a deep voice asked and Sam strolled in, hands dug deeply into pockets. He looked Paula directly in the eye. A fist knotted in her stomach, and she stiffened automatically.

'Nice to see you back, Sam,' Sue said. Looking from one to the other of them, she moved discreetly to the door. 'I'm, er. . .just going to check my list with the girls.'

Dressed in navy jacket and slacks, his black hair was slicked smoothly back and haloed his face—his expression was perhaps a shade tense, the tiny lines of tension creeping out from the dark eyes that held hers. Only the scar across his forehead remained to remind her of what had happened. . .

'How are you feeling?' she managed to ask, avoiding the temptation to tangle with the dark gaze melting over her.

'Pretty good,' he said without expression. 'And you?'

She nodded. 'How's the arm?'

He lifted it. 'As you can see, mobile again.' He paused, frowning. 'Is this all that we have left to say to each other, Paula?' he asked her huskily.

'What do you expect?' she murmured, lifting her eyes. 'If you had anything to tell me—' She stopped, swallowing, trying to calm the anger and hurt inside her. 'All I know is, you lied to me, Sam. And I was fool enough to believe you.'

He caught her arm as she went to turn away. 'I did what?'

'You lied to me—or at least you left something out. That's just as bad.'

He narrowed his eyes, shaking his head. 'This isn't making any sense.'

'What would you have done if I had shown up at the cottage, Sam?' she found herself accusing. 'I should

think my arrival would have been rather embarrassing,
wouldn't it?'

Before he could answer her, she pulled away and
hurried to the door. As she left Sue's room, she saw
one of the girl's showing in her first patient. Discreetly
she wiped the wetness from her lower lid and followed
them, suppressing the sensation that her heart was tearing in two.

CHAPTER TEN

PERHAPS because it was the warmest September in years and the leaves on the trees had already begun to turn a marmalade colour, and the scent of autumn wafted in through the open windows with the last hot breath of summer, Paula sensed all the old ghosts coming back to haunt her.

Emily had died on September the second. Jay had left her six months later and a year after Emily's death, the following September, they had divorced. Within two months, Jay had married again. The fact he had not managed to sustain his attempt at marriage was in no way consolatory to her.

The depression settling over her now, mixed with the bewilderment and disappointment of Sam's unexplained treatment of her, seemed even more mind-blowing than Jay's betrayal.

How could Sam have persuaded her into loving him, led her into trusting him, when he had still been involved with Jilly? Not one word had been said about her—not an attempt at an excuse as to why he had allowed Jilly to collect him from hospital or the reasons for her presence in his life.

And now, Paula reflected sadly, they were polite and distant—Sam absenting himself from her company whenever he could and she doing the same.

Sue and Ken noticed, of course. They tried to heal the obvious breach with jokes and offers of coffee and drinks. The Beeswax for lunch. The house for coffee breaks.

But each of them had found excuses. Mabel and

Poppy seemed too much of a vulnerable area—he must
have at least that much conscience, Paula consoled herself. If Poppy and the pup reminded him of the times
they'd shared this summer. . .

Karen Shore appeared suddenly in her line of vision
and Paula realized she was in the middle of her post-
natal clinic.

'I think he's teething, Dr Harvie,' Karen told her.
Baby James sat on her lap and Paula checked the painful
white areas of gum. He clamped his jaws down on his
tiny fist and sucked.

'I can give you an infant suspension, but I think this
front one's almost through,' Paula told Karen, drawing
her fingers tenderly over the baby's thick cap of
dark hair.

'As long as it's just his teeth,' Karen sighed. 'I've
just been talking to Brenda Vance. She came to your
clinic too in April. Her baby's the same age as James
and he's teething.'

Paula smiled, handing James back. 'Other than the
teething, Karen, he's a nice weight. He's alert, and you
say he's breast-feeding well. He's a lovely baby.'

'My sister says she's coming to you next week for
her first antenatal,' Karen said proudly. 'I suppose
because all I've talked about is your clinic—she
wouldn't want anyone else.'

Paula hesitated. 'I'll be here until November, Karen.
After that, she can transfer to Dr Dunwoody.'

'You're not leaving, are you?' The girl's disappointment was obvious.

Paula shrugged. 'Dr Dunwoody will be ready to take
on antenatal surgeries in November.'

Karen's shoulders slumped. 'I was hoping you'd see
James through to school at least,' she said dis-
appointedly. 'It's not often you find a GP you can relate
to. I really am disappointed.'

Paula realized how disappointed she was, too. She had come, as Sue had said, to have a substantial list of her own. She knew faces now and coupled them each with histories. Even Steven Crane had phoned back to ask for references—a lost cause, she had thought, as she had with Harry Bamford. How wrong she had been. People were beginning to know and trust her. . .

Until this moment she had not let herself think about how attached she'd become to Struan House. The heartache of Sam was bad enough but when it was added to the way she felt about the practice. . .

Dr Carlile's going too, isn't he?' Karen groaned. 'My husband's a patient of his.' Karen struggled up with James and walked to the door. 'Dr Linton's nice, but he's ever so young. Dr Carlile was just right for Darren'.

A conversation which did nothing to cheer Paula up as she saw the last of her patients.

Aunt Steph was equally unhelpful. At supper, she found Paula snivelling over the washing up. She forced her from the sink and wagged a finger at her. 'You miss him, don't you?' She asked, meaning to be kind, but it only made things worse. 'Talk it out. Doesn't love deserve a second chance?'

Paula looked at her aunt in astonishment. 'Love! Aunt Steph—how can you think I love him?'

'I think,' said the older woman slowly, 'you're afraid.'

Paula shook her head determinedly. 'Of love?'

'Of coming to terms with the failure of your marriage—and Emily.'

'But I have come to terms with them!' Paula insisted.

'You began—when I saw your eyes light up for Sam Carlile. Then I knew you were beginning to live again. But you were afraid to go on—'

'With good reason, Aunt Steph. Sam wanted no more than an affair. Perhaps he was trying to get Jilly out of his system. I simply don't know.'

'Don't you think you owe him the benefit of the doubt? After all, there may be a perfectly simple explanation as to what's happened.'

'Aunt Steph, I saw her with my own eyes—and the way he looked at her. Even Ken said Jilly had only to lift her little finger—'

'Ken Dunwoody is an old chatterbox,' her aunt reproved. 'And Sue would be the first to agree. I can't believe Sam would encourage your affections unless he meant to carry things through.'

'It's no use, Aunt Steph. Sam's going back to Delhi. He's even told some of his patients.'

'And you've passed judgement on the word of other people?'

'On what my eyes have seen, Aunt Steph.'

Her aunt put an arm around her shoulders. 'Paula, sometimes it's risky and frightening to tell someone how you feel. For you, there's the space in your life that your father left—neither of you had the opportunity to get to know one another. He was as illusive a figure as Jay was. Compounded with Emily—it's no wonder you're afraid of falling in love and trusting again. But would you really allow that wound to go on festering for the rest of your life without trying one more time? You can't possibly feel any worse than you do now. What harm can there be in talking to Sam?'

Paula sighed, burying her face in a tissue. 'We aren't talking. We're avoiding one another.'

'Then you'll have to make the first move.'

'I can't, Aunt Steph. I can't.'

'You will if you love him.'

'I. . .I don't know—'

'I do,' her aunt sighed. 'And love is worth fighting for.'

*   *   *

Sam, Paula noticed, was dark-eyed—more dark-eyed than usual—heavy rings circled his brown eyes and dulled them. Lines of tension gravitated across his face, he lost his patience easily and she heard him cursing the Mercedes quite volubly one morning when it refused to start.

It was on a September morning, not long after her talk with Aunt Steph, when she collided with him outside the practice. Having plotted their paths so carefully for days in order to avoid each other, they suddenly found themselves confronted, door to door, in the car park.

'Sorry,' he said as he opened his door and his arm brushed hers as she was getting out. 'After you.'

She thought she'd been hit by lightning. A streak of electricity shot up her arm, and she almost fell back against the Polo. 'N. . .no, my fault.'

'Look, it's a bit of a squeeze. . .market day. . .I'll park the Mercedes around the back.'

'No—' Paula reached out. Before she could stop herself she was tugging at his sleeve to stop him from driving away. She looked down, horror-stricken, at her fingers. 'I. . .I mean,' she stammered as she snapped them away, 'there's enough room.'

'No sense in—'

'Oh, for heaven's sake, Sam!' She closed her eyes and put her hand to her head. 'This is absurd. We can't go on like this—as if we were infectious to one another.'

'What do you suggest, then?' He looked at her fiercely. 'I can't leave the damned practice yet—and I don't suppose you can.'

'November,' she gulped, pulling herself together. 'I'm leaving in November.'

'Over month,' he groaned. 'Are we supposed to jump out of each other's way for over a month?'

'It shouldn't be so difficult. . .'

'We're two adults—'

'I. . . I've been meaning to talk to you,' she began, and wished she hadn't. Her face crimsoned and every sensible thought flew out of her mind.

'And I've been waiting—but I didn't think you wanted to.'

She leaned back against the Polo, taking a breath. 'I don't find this easy—'

'Obviously not.' He looked broodingly at her. 'I realize I must have been pushing my luck. . .demanding too much—'

'The truth is, I didn't want an affair, Sam,' she suddenly choked. 'I realize now I must have let you think I did, but it wasn't like that, not really. Aunt Steph said I should be truthful. . .'

'And you haven't been?'

'Not really, no.' She looked up, her eyes moistening dangerously. 'Oh, this is not how I meant to say it. . .'

'Good God, Paula, I wanted you. I thought we had something special.' He raised his arms, the strong white poplin of his shirt straining against the muscle beneath.

She stared at him, amazed that he could still not utter the two words on which this whole discussion rested. Jilly Cameron. It was nothing to do with whether she wanted an affair or not—it was Jilly Cameron. Did he really think, like Jay, that he could carry on two relationships at one time and then start making pathetic excuses?

'Paula, whatever our dilemma, we can't tread on glass for the next few weeks.' He brushed his hand irritably through the dark wing of hair and looked at her. 'And nor can Sue and Ken. They're pretty uptight about us. Ken had a word with me yesterday. It seems the whole practice is aware of what's going on.'

'So what do you suggest we do, Sam?'

'Try to be a little nicer to one another, I suppose.'

She shrugged. 'I don't want to upset Ken or Sue. They've been very good to me.'

'And there's Poppy and Mabel.' He looked to the practice. 'Last night was Mabel's first night at the Dunwoodys'. The cottage seems pretty empty without her and without—'He shrugged, turning slightly to nod towards the surgery. 'Let's try for other people's sakes, shall we?'

So this really was the end? She couldn't remember ever feeling so totally devastated. She'd talked to him and failed. There was nothing else to be said. He would never mention Jilly and nor would she. They would trek through the next few weeks being even more polite to one another.

'I suggest we go in together this morning,' he told her with a shrug. 'Try, at least, for the benefit of the staff.'

She hoisted her bag from the car, trying not to let him see the twist of pain at her mouth, the tears held in check so fiercely her fingers clenched the case with furious desperation.

'Then there's this wedding. . .'

Paula stopped in the middle of locking her car. 'W . . . wedding?' she mumbled. 'What wedding?'

'Had you forgotten? Harry and Janine's. October the fifth. We've all had invitations. I hardly think either one of us could decline without being outrageously obvious.'

Paula swallowed. 'It had slipped my mind.'

'I'll think of an excuse.'

She shook her head. 'No—as you say, it would be too noticeable if either of us was not there.'

He nodded. 'Then we'd better make the best of it.'

She pulled back her shoulders and dredged up a smile. 'Yes. I suppose we had.'

'Can you see your way to coming in my car?'

She began to protest and then stopped. What did it matter whose car? What did anything matter any more?

All she had to try to do was stumble through the next few weeks without totally disintegrating. 'If you really think it necessary.' She sighed.

'I do, from Ken and Sue's point of view. I told Ken Poppy could come with us. I couldn't think of anything else to say. He hinted at it and I felt obliged to say yes.'

She looked tiredly towards the surgery. 'Well, we'd better go in.'

He stood back and gestured for her to walk between the two cars. She forced herself onward, aware of him moving silently beside her, of the attraction of his tall body as she braced herself to walk into the practice and put on a brave smile. She would know, even if she had her eyes closed, who it was who walked beside her. If he stood across the other side of the street staring at her, she would still know, even though her back was turned, that he was there.

'After you,' he said as he pressed open the door with a firm brown hand. A cascade of chills swept over her spine as her gaze flicked over the five strong, beautiful fingers. . .

'Morning!' he called as they walked in. She smiled beside him, waving to the girls who watched them from Reception. Her body treacherously ached as he slipped an arm around her waist in a friendly gesture, looking down to meet her eyes with an expression of familiarity which would have been solely reserved for her—or so she would have thought once, in her innocence, not knowing about Jilly Cameron.

Weddings were not her strong point.

She had long since ceased to become excited at the thought of a church wedding. Five long years of attending other people's on her own had taken the magic out of it for her. Weddings were wonderful if you were in love, too. She remembered how she had felt when she had gone to several during her marriage. With Jay by her side she had believed in the myth and mystery and had lapped up every nuance.

Looking back, it had seemed her happiness had been impregnable and no other man had matched Jay. His blond good looks were a pale second to Sam's dark and chiselled features, but women had found him charming and attractive, as she had found out to her cost just before giving birth to Emily.

'Come along, dear,' Aunt Steph said, snapping her fingers and bringing Paula out of her reverie. They were standing in Warwick town centre, in a discreet little boutique where Aunt Steph had dragged her to buy a new outfit. 'It makes you look too pale,' her aunt said of the navy blue dress Paula thought she had settled on half an hour ago.

'Oh, it just needs a scarf.' Paula sighed, uninterestedly. 'And I'll probably not wear it again for ages. It will do.'

'You've lost weight,' her aunt grumbled. 'I knew you hadn't been eating.'

'Like a horse,' Paula countered. 'I'll just pay—'

'Try this,' Aunt Steph persuaded gently, taking an expensive-looking suit from a rail. 'Just for me. This last one.'

Paula sighed, took the suit and changed in the little room. The assistant poked her head around the door. 'Oh! Gorgeous!'

For the first time, Paula studied herself. She had lost weight, and she'd been trying to fool herself that she hadn't, but the two-piece did something to her figure which the dress didn't, filling in the gaps, smoothing over her waist and moulding her hips in pencil-slim elegance. The skirt was cut above the knee—the colour was the palest of greys which matched her eyes and suddenly made them look alive, and the softly scooped neckline under which the silk top cleaved gently to her breasts seemed made for her shape.

She came out to show Aunt Steph.

'Darling, it's perfect,' gasped Aunt Steph.

'But it's shockingly expensive and I probably won't wear it again.'

'Rubbish,' her aunt spluttered. 'Treat yourself.'

'It really is lovely,' agreed the assistant.

'Well. . .' debated Paula, looking back at the navy blue dress.

'All we need now,' said her aunt energetically, 'are shoes and a hat.'

'No!' Paula protested, fleeing to the changing room. 'No more! I'm exhausted. I'll have this.' She whipped off the suit and emerged in her jeans and sweater, and found Aunt Stephanie looking through the window at the shoe shop opposite.

'Absolutely not,' said Paula firmly. 'I'm shattered.'

But by the end of the day she had bought a new suit, a pair of exquisitely fashionable and expensive pale grey shoes and tiny pearl earrings. She had dug her heels in over the hat!

The wedding of Harry Bamford took place as arranged at the tiny chapel of Saint Benedict's. The October day, could have been August, with a melting sun and thirst-making vibrations of warm, dry breezes.

Sam came to collect her before picking up Poppy. He looked breathtaking. He wore a dark, flawless suit, and his hair had just been cut, sweeping back across his head and lying softly at the nape of his neck, so glossy and healthy-looking that the first moment Paula saw it she had the aching sensation of wanting to run her fingers through it.

His dark eyes still showed the essence of tiredness and the grey shadows were still there. If she hadn't known him as she did, she would have thought he hadn't a care in the world. But she realized this must be as much of a pressure to him as it was to her.

He stood still at the door for one moment, staring at her. She'd taken her time with the suit and shoes, showering and dressing carefully, suddenly wanting to look better than ever before. Better than Jilly Cameron? she'd taunted herself as she'd looked in the full-length mirror.

Her hair had grown whilst she'd been at the practice. It now fell in a long, thick bob to her shoulders, and it gleamed healthily, spilling out softly to kiss the grey material of her suit. Her fairness and her grey eyes complemented the material—Aunt Steph had been right. But for a moment, as he scrutinized her, she wondered. . .

'You look beautiful,' he told her in that rich, dark voice which melted her bones, his eyes seeming to pierce through her clothes to her skin. 'Very beautiful, Paula.'

'Thank you,' she mumbled, and changed the subject. 'I'm ready. I've just the wedding gift. . .'

He followed her in. In the small front room, she picked up the box she had wrapped neatly in wedding paper and decorated with tiny silver bells.

'Let me,' he said, taking it from her. His fingers covered her own, and she jumped, her eyes going up to meet his, and in that second she couldn't move.

'I've bought a coffee percolator,' she said, gulping. 'One of those new ones advertised on television—

He smiled slowly. 'Snap. So have I.'

'You haven't?'

'I have.' He laughed softly, a noise which made her shiver, sending little currents of pleasure through her body as his fingers still covered her own.

'It can't be the same. . .'

'I'll bet it is.'

For a moment she felt transported—his smile and

laughter and the pleasure he was giving her as his fingers moved lightly across hers—then her heart lurched haphazardly as he took the box and moved it to the table, then turned and slid his hands around her waist, almost as though she had been waiting for him to take her in his arms.

'Oh, Paula,' he whispered. 'Paula. . .'

'Sam, don't,' she protested, wanting him more than she had ever wanted anyone in her life. And yet how could she? He was in love with someone else—he had hurt her. . .

His lips came down and captured hers, and her body shuddered against him. She clung helplessly to his strong arms, his ravaged face telling her how much he wanted her as their eyes locked, and the kiss smouldered over her lips. A tear slid from her eye and he kissed it away, his lips smoothing over her skin.

'Oh, Sam. . .' she breathed, and her voice trailed into nothing.

He kissed her again and she choked back the emotion building inside her as his tongue probed the sweetness of her mouth and the secret, intimate places of arousal. After an age he lifted his head and gazed into her eyes, and she knew if they didn't have the wedding to go to she would have given way as his arms tightened around her and she accepted the warmth and comfort of his embrace without protest.

'Where do we go from here, my love?' he said softly, and she shook her head.

'I don't know,' she mumbled, her fingers tingling as she drifted them across his shoulders. 'I don't know what's happening any more.'

'I know I want you more than anything,' he whispered, clasping her face in his hands. 'I have always wanted you.'

'Even when you thought I was Jilly?' There. Her heart almost stopped. She had said it.

'Jilly?' He frowned. 'What has Jilly got to do with us?'

Her eyes filled with tears. 'Everything. Sam, I saw you that day at the hospital. I know you're still in love with her.'

'Paula.' He held her out from him, frowning. 'Paula, do you know what you're saying?'

'I saw you, Sam,' she repeated in a choked voice. 'And I waited for you to tell me. . . I'd seen her on the video at the cottage, and upstairs there's a bottle in your bathroom,' she gulped, unable to stop the flow. 'And when you went to London I knew you didn't want me to phone you at her place, and then you were beside her in the Porsche—'

Just then Aunt Steph called from the back door. Sam cursed under his breath but let her go. She quickly dabbed at her smudged mascara with a tissue whilst he walked away and prowled the room.

At the back door Aunt Steph gazed at her. 'Oh, darling, I just wanted to see how you looked.'

Paula blushed and pressed down her skirt, her thoughts in turmoil.

'Beautiful of course.' Aunt Steph sighed, echoing Sam's words. She leaned to kiss Paula on the cheek. 'Have a happy day—and say hello to Sam for me.'

Then she was gone, and Paula dragged herself back into the house. Sam was standing against the light of the window, his large frame silhouetted.

'Aunt Steph says hello,' Paula mumbled, and grabbed her bag, unable to meet his gaze after her outburst. Now he would see just how hopelessly jealous she'd been. Now he would see right into her soul.

'I. . .I think it's time we went,' she stammered.

'It always is,' Sam said in a hard voice.

And without a word, he strode out of the house to the car.

CHAPTER ELEVEN

JANINE was given away by her father in the flagstoned, flower-filled chapel of St Benedict's. Harry looked a new man, standing tall and erect by her side. Janine wore a creamy satin gown and Harry a formal black coat and a top-hat.

The couple's friends included the slimming group and all the staff from Struan House who sat in quiet admiration of the tranquil service. Only Poppy who sat in between Sam and Paula insisted on peering out from the pew into the aisle. Sam brought her back and sat her on his knee, and Sue turned around and gave her a motherly frown, putting a finger to her mouth.

Paula thought how lovely Sue looked in a soft pink dress and coat, and Ken slid his arm around his wife's waist, obviously remembering their own wedding day. She struggled not to think of her own. And to her surprise it was there, but tucked away like a necklace in cotton wool. She couldn't remember Jay's face clearly or the sound of his voice—but she could remember Sam's.

She didn't need to look at him to know he was there. Once again his presence reached her, over the top of Poppy's head, drawing her towards him as though she were metal to his magnet.

Oh, Sam, she cried inside. I wanted this. I wanted this for us—and I was too scared. I was a coward. I couldn't tell you. I was afraid of losing you. And I have lost you. I couldn't fight her. She was too strong. . .

Paula gulped and tried to concentrate on the music as it wafted joyfully up into the beams. Everyone threw confetti and laughed and scrambled to take photos. They

179

grouped outside, and Sam brought out the camcorder
and took miles of film. Whilst Paula was watching with
Poppy and trying to look happy, a tall young man wearing spectacles came hurrying across the grass.

'Selwyn!' gasped Paula, hauling Poppy into her arms.
'What are you doing here? Do you know the Bamfords?'

He laughed. 'Hello, Dr Harvie. No, I don't, but I play
the organ for the chapel, didn't you know?'

Paula shook her head. 'It was beautiful music,
Selwyn.'

'As a matter of fact, we're coming to see you next
month.' Before Paula could explain she might not be
there he hurried on. 'Sally and I are hoping to foster a
child—maybe even adopt. Sally wasn't enthusiastic at
first. . .after Louise.' His voice gave a little hitch but he
swallowed and went on. 'What you said helped. She
didn't feel as if she was the only one who'd lost a baby.
And she kept up with the counselling. Through the social
worker we were advised of our options. The thing is,
we think we'd like to offer an older child a home. There
are lots, apparently, who'll never have the opportunity
of belonging to a real family. People prefer babies.' He
shrugged. 'Anyway, we might need your help—they do
very thorough checks.'

'I'll be glad to give it, but I don't think I'll—'

Just then, Sam appeared by her side. Selwyn retold
his story, and Sam shook him by the hand. 'Just let us
know what we can do for you.'

Sam took Poppy from Paula's arms as Selwyn left
and threw her over his shoulder. She screamed in delight.

Paula's heart gave a tug. 'I won't be able to do much
for Selwyn and Sally,' she said, forcing back the lump
in her throat. 'Unless they can manage to reach me
wherever I am.'

'And where will that be?' Sam asked abruptly.

Paula looked down at her hands. 'I'm not sure.'

'So you're running away again?'

'No!' She stuck out her chin and glared at him. 'You accused me of running away the very first day we met.'

'And aren't you running away again?'

'No. . . I. . . I. . .'

Sam ignored her completely and lowered Poppy gently to the ground. She sat on his foot and giggled. He ruffled her hair, and slid an arm around Paula's waist. 'They've the reception at the Beeswax,' he told her as he tugged her towards him 'We're going to show our faces for half an hour and then we're going back to the cottage.'

'The cottage?' She frowned, but he silenced her by sliding his mouth over her lips in full view of everyone, and especially to Poppy's uproarious amusement.

They gave one coffee percolator between them and Paula went scarlet. She promised herself she would buy something else in the week and apologize by letter. Sam devoured a plate of creative little Beeswax pastries, and they said goodbye to the Dunwoodys who had to return home to relieve Mrs McDuff of Jeremy.

When they had gone, Sam caught her hand. 'Say goodbye to the happy couple. We're disappearing.'

'But, Sam—'

'Do as you're told. I'll be waiting in the car.'

She did as she was bade, and Harry and his beautiful bride thanked them both for coming. She slunk away, hoping no one would notice.

Sam had the engine of the car running. She gazed at his face as she belted up, trying to read his expression. It was implacable. He said nothing until they arrived at the cottage. And then it was only four words as he swept her into his arms and growled, 'You silly little witch.'

He almost air-lifted her into the cottage. He dragged her after him and into the front room. Taking the video marked Delhi, he slapped it onto the coffee table, making her jump. Then, clasping her hand tightly, he pulled her up the stairs to the bathroom. He scrabbled amongst the debris on the shelves and came up with the perfume bottle. He dragged her downstairs again to the front room where he pushed her down onto the sofa and lowered the perfume atomizer beside the video. He brought in the answer machine and crashed it next to the other items on the coffee table.

'Item one,' he said, and tapped the bottle with a heavy finger. 'Leftovers from the wretched woman I bought the cottage from. There's half a dozen others like it somewhere—I'm surprised you didn't find them when you raided my drawers.'

He cast the video into her lap 'Item two. Sure, it's Jilly. After we broke up. No doubt scheming the best way to pull the plug on me at the unit. She favoured the place being turned into some kind of medical Disneyland for the benefit of her new boyfriend. And it almost happened, too—if I hadn't managed to find Lorimar.'

'Sam, I—'

'Item three. Answer machine. Ancient and needs replacing. Makes mistakes. Needs encouragement. Listen!' He pushed the button several times, shook it and then rattled it on the table. Finally his own voice came over—the message he said he'd left, from the hospital, asking her to collect him as soon as she could.

'Oh, Sam, I didn't think to check—'

'If I had known the damn thing was going to get me into all this trouble I'd have chucked it out long ago.'

Paula stared at the answer machine, shaking her head. 'I thought when I saw Jilly at the hospital—'

'I know what you thought.'

'It was so easy to believe you still loved her.'

He lifted a dark eyebrow. 'Paula, whatever there was

between Jilly and I was over long ago. All Jilly wanted to do was to tell me she's moving to the States. She tracked me down from one of the girls at Reception— to be honest, I was so damn mad with you, whatever she told me went in one ear and out the other. I couldn't believe you'd let me languish in that hell-hole all day!'

Paula hesitated, her brow caught in a frown. 'But if she's not going back to India. . .?'

He shrugged. 'It makes no odds to me. Long ago I decided it was time to offload the responsibility of the unit to someone else. Lorimar came up with a team of medics of their own—all part of the package deal I was negotiating in London. I decided it was time for me to come home—there was the offer from Sue and Ken to partner them in practice—it was very tempting—and then, of course, there was you.'

Paula stared at him incredulously. 'But when I asked them Ken and Sue seemed so sure you were set on returning to India.'

'Why didn't you ask me?' He grinned, and stood up and pulled her to her feet. 'I would have told you all you wanted to know.'

'Oh, Sam—I couldn't. I was afraid of the answer, I think.'

'Well,' he murmured softly, 'let me convince you now, Dr Harvie. . .' He drew her from the room and towards the stairs, and she followed obediently, her heart skipping raggedly. He took her to his room and closed the door, then he drew her into his arms and kissed her, taking hungry possession of her mouth as he reached out and began to unbutton her jacket.

He worked out her arms from the sleeve, drawing the soft grey material from her skin and cast it onto the chair. Then he reached around her waist and slid down the zip of her skirt, easing the rest of it over her hips until it fell around her heels and she kicked it out of the way.

'Oh, Sam, I don't know what to say. . .' His fingers plucked at the silky white teddy and he slid it over her head, staring with dark brown eyes at her breasts rising quickly under a lacy white bra.

'Don't say anything. Just let me look at you.' He tilted her chin to search her eyes as his gaze feasted over her body, and he took her by the arms and laid her gently down on the bed.

'Your turn,' he said, and guided her fingers to his shirt and tie which she slipped off from his body, her excitement mounting as she ran her fingers over the hard muscle and smooth dark skin and down across his hips.

His face was tense with longing, his eyes roved hungrily over her once more as he brought her hands to his waist and she tugged him down beside her, her heart beating with all the pent-up passion which lay inside her.

Then he was lying against her and she struggled with his shorts, and he moaned at the back of his throat. 'You're so very beautiful, my love,' he groaned, and cupped her breasts as he released her bra, freeing her breasts from their feather-light casing, bending to kiss and tease them as the small dark buds of desire responded achingly to the first stroke of his agile tongue.

She cried his name, closing her eyes, melting into his body, limbs and arms entangled, hearts pounding, lips searching. With a soft, husky moan she leaned her head back on the pillow and let him possess her. She discovered everything he did she loved: the way he bit and sucked and soothed her, his teasing tongue, the places she could not imagine aroused becoming aroused; even her toenails and knees were throbbing.

'Turn over,' he whispered, and she cradled against him trustingly. He ran his tongue over her shoulders, kneading the sensitive muscles of her neck with his thumbs, drawing a line down her spine with a finger so that she stiffened and gasped and his hands slid around her hips and drew her into him.

He was wholly and devastatingly male, legs, arms and hips at a perfect juxtaposition to her own as he turned her in his arms, the curls of dark hair on his chest seductively grazing her sensitized breasts.

She gazed down into his face, her hair falling over them both, and he tugged it with his teeth until he collided with her nose and kissed her until they pulled away laughing, only to gasp for air and then tangle once more in the sheets.

When their play ended, their lovemaking began. She fell headlong into the world of fantasy, of human warmth and stimulation, of loving and being loved as she had never been loved before.

'Let me. . .' he whispered and she lay in his arms, a tide of eroticism sweeping over her body at his command as his fingers carefully played her.

'Oh, Sam,' she whispered as his body covered her, and she cried out again.

'Wait, my love,' he coaxed, and she waited, knowing he would lead her, show her the way. 'I want to make this last for ever. For ever. . .'

Her shuddering reply was lost in the sensual flowering of a love which she knew would last all her life. Slowly, beguilingly, at last shackled to him by the power of this love, she opened the gate to her heart and soul.

He possessed her with quickening passion, delighting in the wonder of her body as she gave herself wholly to him, his fire warming the embers of her glowing desire as they hurtled together to the climax of their love.

Many hours later, Sam curved a lean hand across her cheek, bringing her mouth to his as she moved into his arms, laying her head in the crook of his shoulder.

'You're all I've ever wanted, Paula,' he whispered against her ear. 'I want you with me for the rest of our lives.'

Suffused in a warm glow of contentment, she smoothed her fingers lovingly over the firm, grainy skin of his arms as they wrapped tightly around her. 'A future means a family. . .' she whispered. 'Do you want children, Sam?'

'I want you and I want to be able to remember Emily with you. To be able to go with you to visit her first. . . so we can make her memory part of us. Then. . .' His voice, a deep, husky murmur, evoked a lump in her throat as she nodded, touched by his understanding and compassion, which made her love him all the more.

'Sam, I want babies of our own, too,' she whispered. 'I want a family.' In her heart she knew that Sam would be there for her, would always be there for her. And that all her concerns and fears would be shared and that she could face the memory of Emily's loss.

Her hands moved over his body in a rush of warmth, and she turned into his chest as her eyes moved up to the dark and handsome face as he bent down to kiss her, whispering sweet words of love and desire.

Their passion stirred again as she wrapped herself into his long, lean body, and the wanton ache of longing began to awaken once more and stir them into a yearning wakefulness, as a small smile touched his lips, his eyes dancing over the curve of her open mouth. 'And there will be the practicalities,' he said softly, his eyes teasing. 'We've three bedrooms. . .I could have the nursery ready for July. . .'

'July?'

'And a November wedding gives us time to settle down for Christmas.'

'Sam—'

'We've lain in this bed enjoying ourselves for the last twelve hours,' he reminded her unnecessarily. 'And we've another six to go before either of us has to get up.' He kissed her again, cradling her face in his tender hands as she stared up into his eyes, certain now of the total commitment she was prepared to give and that he knew it too, as the loving pleasures of bed involved their hearts and bodies in the solid contract of love.

'Pink napkins,' Paula mused as Sam came up behind her and wrapped his arms around her waist. The smell of coffee wafted through the kitchen and the breakfast table was set for two. 'Pink napkins. . .'

He arched an eyebrow, smirking as he nestled his lips in the crook of her neck, watching the last forlorn pink napkin wrap slowly through her fingers. 'Want to know who they were for?' Before she could reply, he turned her to face him and stared into the inscrutable concern of her worried eyes.

'I had it all planned,' he admitted with a wry smile, 'for a certain young woman whom was expecting to call and whom I wanted to impress. But it all misfired because of that blasted atomizer.'

'You mean, the meal was for me?'

'It took me hours to concoct that salmon. . .'

She began to laugh, reaching up on tiptoe to kiss him, winding her arms around his neck as she felt the strength and power melt her again, her body growing warm with a fresh surge of melting desire.

'In future,' he whispered as he brushed the hair from her face and looked deeply into her eyes, 'the kitchen's all yours, my sweet.'

She nestled happily into his arms. 'I've a job to go to, remember?'

'Not for much longer.'

She smiled secretively. 'Sue's hinted she'd like me to stay.'

'Oh, she did, did she?'

'And now—in view of the circumstances—I'm seriously considering it.'

He grinned above her. 'Then you'll be working with the new partner. I just hope there's not a personality clash. Some say he's like a bear with a sore head.'

She frowned, trying to ignore the sensation he was evoking as he drew a finger over the soft outline of her breast under the towelling robe. 'What new partner?'

'The one who's taking John's place.'

'But John isn't leaving—is he?'

He nodded, lifting wise eyebrows. 'John's wife has been offered a job with a London legal practice—very prestigious, so I hear. They've decided to move to the city—which is why Ken and I put our heads together yesterday.'

Her eyes misted with gentle amusement. 'So tell me, just what is this master plan?'

He snuggled her into him, trapping her in his arms, miraculously folding them both into one human form. 'We thought the Doctors Dunwoody and Carlile should merge. Four doctors of a like mind. . .'

He looked at her innocently and she curled into him, sighing, her eyes fluttering closed. 'Dr Carlile,' she murmured weakly, breathing in the delicious early-morning aroma of his skin against her cheek, 'is there anything else you'd like to confess before you plan the rest of our lives?'

'Mmm,' he whispered as he kissed her into silence. 'But it's not for the single professional woman's consumption.'—and as she scrambled to punish him, he held her ever closer.

'You're impossible,' she told him as his mouth covered hers and she willingly surrendered. 'But I adore you.'

'It's mutual,' he growled. 'Now come here. . .'

4 FREE

books and a surprise gift!

We would like to take this opportunity to thank you for reading this Mills & Boon® book by offering you the chance to take FOUR more specially selected titles from the Medical Romance™ series absolutely FREE! We're also making this offer to introduce you to the benefits of the Reader Service™—

- ★ FREE home delivery
- ★ FREE gifts and competitions
- ★ FREE monthly newsletter
- ★ Books available before they're in the shops
- ★ Exclusive Reader Service discounts

Accepting these FREE books and gift places you under no obligation to buy, you may cancel at any time, even after receiving your free shipment. Simply complete your details below and return the entire page to the address below. *You don't even need a stamp!*

YES! Please send me 4 free Medical Romance books and a surprise gift. I understand that unless you hear from me, I will receive 4 superb new titles every month for just £2.30 each, postage and packing free. I am under no obligation to purchase any books and may cancel my subscription at any time. The free books and gift will be mine to keep in any case.

M8XE

Ms/Mrs/Miss/Mr ....Initials ....
BLOCK CAPITALS PLEASE

Surname ....

Address ....

....

....Postcode...................................

Send this whole page to:
THE READER SERVICE, FREEPOST, CROYDON, CR9 3WZ
(Eire readers please send coupon to: P.O. BOX 4546, DUBLIN 24.)

MILLS & BOON®

Medical Romance™

COMING NEXT MONTH

DEFINITELY MAYBE by Caroline Anderson

Audley Memorial   *'where romance is the best medicine'*

Ben felt he was making progress; Tassy wasn't just saying 'no' anymore, now she was saying 'maybe', and not just 'maybe' but *'definitely maybe'*!

WANTING DR WILDE by Lilian Darcy

Enemies and Lovers

They owned rival practices but they were also attracted to each other. Francesca *had* to convince Luke that they were on the same side.

A GROWING TRUST by Sheila Danton

With trust they could be the perfect family

Jess was pleased that Andrew was fond of her daughter but she was beginning to question what he really wanted—her or a ready made family?

TALL, D'ARC AND TEMPTING by Margaret Holt

Loving and giving...

Jenny was *tempted* by Findlay D'Arc but how could she compete with the memory of his adorable Gabriella?

On Sale from **1st June 1998**

Available at most branches of WH Smith, John Menzies, Martins, Tesco, Volume One and Safeway